One of a Kind

By

Belinda Topan

Second printing edition 2024

ISBN:

www.belindatopan.com.au

Facebook: www.facebook.com/belindatopan/

Instagram: @belindatopan

Acknowledgments

This project is supported by the Regional Arts Development Fund (RADF). RADF is a partnership between the Queensland Government and Logan City Council to support arts and culture in regional Queensland.

TurtlePublishing

Book Cover design & Editing by Turtle Publishing.

https://turtlepublishing.com.au/

Chapters

Thank you

To my friends, my family, my beta readers, readers and fellow authors. Thank you all so much for your support and the patience you have endured waiting, beta reading, and supporting me for a new book.

Seeing you at conventions, markets, has been a joy and I love talking to you all and I can't wait to do it all over again!

I hope you enjoy this new title and hope you like this crazy story and the world I have created.

To my family, thank you for sticking by me and putting up with my doomsday thoughts haha.

To Mum,

I did it. My fourth book. I wish you were here to celebrate with me. But I know you would be incredibly proud. <3

Prologue

Life, so warm, sweet, fragile, and bright. It slips through your fingers as death's icy grasp tightens around your throat, draining your body's warmth. Oh, little lamb, did you truly believe you could elude me? It's almost amusing, your thoughts of escape, hiding up here, believing you'd lost me. Yet, unwittingly, you trapped yourself. Your chance has slipped away; life flows from your veins, feeding my insatiable hunger, plunging me into a blissful stupor. Your heart slows, each beat duller than the last. Fresh salty tears trickle down your face, smudging the eyeliner you took so long to apply, leaving messy black streaks. Foolish little mouse.

Dark whispers croon sweet nothings into my ear, urging me to continue. I pay them no heed. They are mere servants, eager for another soul to join their ranks.

I hear light footsteps approach and feel their gaze linger on the back of my head. I pay no mind to the figure behind me as I feed upon my dinner. They know how little I hunt, even in all my years. I still enjoy the chase, the thrill, the taste that is something that will never die away. These joys will never fade.

"Odd place for a meal," the figure speaks with a hint of jest in their tone. Detaching from the lifeless body, I let pleasure wash over me, feeling the rejuvenation from tonight's feast. I lick the remaining blood off my lips, my fangs retracting. The body falls onto the concrete with a thud, and I turn to my brother with a welcoming smile. His eyes, reflecting the moonlight, don't hold questions or judgments, but an understanding.

Hawkeye, who doesn't go by his real name, is a tall gentleman with light brown hair, neatly tied back with a black ribbon. A nod to old-fashioned tastes.

"She ran all the way up here. Quite thoughtful, really, as I enjoy dinner with a view." I gaze back at the cityscape, admiring the tall towers and street lights below.

Hawkeye laughs, slapping his hand on my shoulder. "Rather thoughtful of her."

"Any news from Killer?" We both survey the cityscape.

"No, Scar is awaiting his response," Hawkeye replies.

"What about me?" We turn to find Killer scaling the side of the building.

The most muscular among us, his hair short on all sides, and short fringe spiked upwards with gel to defy gravity.

"You could've taken the stairs," Hawkeye chortles. Killer merely shrugs, approaching us.

"It's quicker to climb," he grunts, crossing his arms. I smile at my brothers' banter, their interaction always amusing. Hawkeye notices. Any smile from me is rare and rewarding to the younger vampire.

"Did you and Scar discover anything?" I interject. They pause, and Killer's mouth forms an 'o', reminding himself of his purpose.

"Scar is dealing with the aftermath now," Killer answers. I frown at this news.

"Aftermath? You were to meet the warlock for information." Killer shakes his head.

"We arrived, and the pungent scent of blood overwhelmed us," He growls, his eyes dulling to grey. "Entering, we found the warlock bound to a chair, a bullet through his skull." His gaze fixated on the concrete roof. I sigh, pinching the bridge of my nose.

"We'll undoubtedly be blamed for this," I remove my hand from my face. "Go and get someone to eat, Killer." He nods and departs by leaping off the building's edge.

"Should we worry?" Hawkeye inquires. I stare back at the cityscape as the wind picks up.

"We'll stay vigilant, but let's hope not. The last thing we need is a war within the magical community."

"Everyone despises us. What's one more race to add to the list?" Hawkeye jests. I remain silent; his joke might amuse some, but this is serious. Noting my silence, he sighs. "Things will turn out fine. We'll stay alert." I nod, slightly reassured.

"Whatever the warlock wanted to convey was crucial. We must discern if this will have repercussions for our kind."

"We'll resolve this," he assures, placing a hand on my shoulder and squeezing.

"I hope you're right."

Chapter 1

Nestled between the towering red brick buildings of the school, the wide open paths of the campus became an unexpected arena. The midday sun shone blindingly bright, and the heat sizzling my skin as I stand under its harsh rays.

With no teachers in sight and the usual bustle of the lunch crowed, everyone watched from afar. Not daring to get near for the fear of getting caught up in the altercation, but close enough to watch in eager anticipation to see who would win.

A motley crew of towering figures, with sneers and smirks, encircle me. Ignoring the poor soul, they originally picked as their target. The familiar scent of freshly fallen rain in mountain forests mixed with damp soil and wood, running rivers, and burly waterfalls calms my senses every time I breathe in the clean air. This scent is a little off, though. Rain oddly followed by an overbearing scent, hidden, masked. It's as if someone is burning sugar. Something in me niggles in the back of my head, telling me this is important.

His long black raven bangs hang in front, shaping his sharp face and the back is short and spiked.

I recognise the familiar burn of anger flash across his hazel eyes. He shakes his head at me, slowly.

I step forward and shrug off my old friend's warning and position myself with a silent challenge. The air thickened with tension, the sounds of the school fading into a distant murmur.

I breathe out, throwing off the hideous blue hat, removing the small multicoloured tie from my white blouse and thank my morning self for putting tights on. Flashing half the school is the last thing I want to do.

Time slows around me. A group of jocks circles like a pack of hyenas, pepped up on a volatile mix of adrenaline and testosterone. Their feet tap-dance on the ground as a chorus of slurs and insults dribble out like venom. They seem eager yet hesitant, eyeing one another, wondering who will make the first move.

Finally, the first fist flies towards me. White knuckles cleave through the air, but to me, this is nothing more than a breeze. Slow and manageable, I duck, fingers coiling around his wrist, and with a fluid motion, I hurl him towards his friends. A tangle of bodies and cries arise from the group.

Another boy, blinded by rage, charges at me from behind. I pivot, facing him, and seize his arm. With a twist and a pull, I send him down to the ground. A loud, unforgiving smack against his back steals the air from his lungs. The boy wheezes and gasps, desperate for breath.

A third one attempts to tackle me; his strategy is as obvious as a goanna raiding a nice family picnic. Predictable. I sidestep and watch as he gracelessly charges into a steel pole. A resounding clang echoes as he knocks himself out. He falls to the ground with a heavy thud. The corners of my lips rise, a cruel satisfaction blossoming in my chest at the sight of the boy lying on the ground.

Suddenly, weight clings onto my back– like a spider monkey. Sausage-like fingers grip my face, suffocating the air from my lungs. Instinct takes over. My teeth sink deep into their flesh. The taste of iron floods my mouth, and the tang of blood, so vile, sends tremors through me. The boy recoils from me, holding onto his bleeding hand for dear life. All colour drains from his face, eyes widening in fear as he sees the birth of a monster.

I spit the blood out and wipe away the stains. With a feral snarl, I lunge at the injured boy. My fist connects with his cheek, and the satisfying sound of bone cracking against my knuckles resonates. His head snaps back, his body failing him as he crashes back onto the concrete, hitting the ground with finality.

The remaining boys edge around, jerking back and forth in a dance of indecision and fear. They glance at one another, all sharing the unspoken question: Do we fight or run? With a glare, fury ignites in my veins. "Fuck off."

They take off, running in various directions, desperate to escape the wrath they have unleashed upon themselves. Their footsteps fade away, and I am left alone. Adrenaline slowly ebbs away, and the desire to break bones leaves me feeling hollow.

I walk up to the dishevelled teen in front of me. The familiar smell of freshly fallen rain, the ebony hair hiding his hazel eyes.

"You okay?" I ask, kneeling in front of him. He looks at me, a burning fury hiding behind his bangs.

"You shouldn't have stepped in." My old friend winces and grabs his ribs. I sigh and ignore his warning. Offering my hand, I wait for him to take it.

"Come with me, Zack." He stares at my hand for what seemed like a minute and finally takes it. Lifting him to his feet, we leave the small group to lick their wounds and moan in pain as we exit the scene.

The school grounds, usually a place of mundane daily routines, had transformed momentarily into a battleground, and now, seeking solace and a quiet spot for Zack to recover, I know exactly where to go.

Weaving through the familiar pathways of the school, we make our way to a less frequented part of the campus. The auditorium, with its large, imposing doors usually locked after school hours, looms ahead. It's a place of rehearsals, assemblies, and the occasional drama class, but during hours, it offers the quiet and privacy we need.

I take Zack to the back of the auditorium, and tuck ourselves away by the metal roller doors. Hidden away from prying eyes. I gently sit him down on the concrete and kneel beside him. The light filtering through the tree branches, giving us enough shade from the harsh sun as the recent event begins to settle in. He remains silent as I assess his injuries.

"You're going to get into trouble, you know that, right?" He winces as I touch the cut on his cheek. It isn't deep, thankfully; it should heal in a few days.

"I know," I move his bang to his ear and looking at the bruise on his right eye.

"You should have walked away."

"And watch you get beaten to a pulp?"

"I told you to stay away from me."

"I have!" I snap. "You've been staying away from me." Zack looks away in shame. "Telling me we're not friends. Not giving me an explanation and keeping me in the dark."

"I have my reasons," Zack give a long pause before speaking again. "Next time, stay away." Fury bubbles to the surface. A burning rage grows in my chest. I grab his shirt and crash him into the wall. Pain throbs in my upper jaw. The burning in my veins intensifies.

"I don't fucking get it. What did I do wrong, Zack? Why won't you talk to me!" Zack becomes a wall, his head to the side, hiding behind his bangs and looking away from my gaze. The grimace of unsaid words holds them back in fear; will he finally spill the truth? I clench my teeth. The fury bubbling to the surface and the desire to bite and inflict pain grows. I suppress the desire and take a deep breath. "I just wish you would tell me," Hoping this would spill his guts.

Heavy steps approach us both, and the vice principal stands before us with her hands on her hips.

"Let him go, Ceres!"

In the office foyer, the aftermath of the fight unfolds like a tense drama. The jocks' parents, the principal, vice principal, and Zack's mother all stand like wallflowers. All are afraid to approach one another. Each parent scrutinises the injuries of the three boys, while the rest comfort their children with tight embraces. I stand in the corner, watching, the ache in my chest expanding as I ponder what it's like to have someone worry for me like that, to have a parent leap to my defence.

I pretend to ignore them and let my gaze wonder over to our year twelve class photo taken three months ago. The bold numbers '2013' glittering in the light. I stare down at the fake cheerful smile I present within the glass frame.

All the mothers from the group unite and hurl accusations at Zack and his mother, asserting their child is a 'good boy who would never initiate a fight.' Zack's mother, her eyes tired and ringed with dark circles, looks more defeated than angry. She glances at me, her gaze heavy with unasked questions and unspoken understanding.

"What happened, Ceres?" her voice is soft but laden with a weight to ground me from my thoughts. I open my mouth to speak, to explain, but before I can respond. Doors swing open with a dramatic thud, silencing the room. Zack gives the man approaching a lethal glare.

The mothers murmur among themselves. Listening in on their conversation, they speak of how the man brings an air of authority about him. Their gazes linger on his striking appearance, from the subtle nods and raised eyebrows. His bright blonde hair is perfectly slicked back, a pristine white shirt and jacket on top with black slacks. I scrunch my nose in disdain at his outfit; he resembles a dodgy real-estate agent, a facade of charm hiding something less savoury.

"Mr. Treacher, thank you for meeting with us at such short notice," the principal greets. My gut twists, knowing the name and the trademark charming smile. My guardian, Nic.

He removes his sunglasses, revealing his piercing blue eyes. I watch in the corner, Nic's demeanour poised and professional, and greet the principal with a warm, yet firm handshake. Despite my annoyance, I can't help but begrudgingly acknowledge his ability to command respect in any situation. It's a quality I've witnessed countless times during these 'meetings' and as much as I resent it, I have to admit, it's impressive.

"It's no trouble at all. I deeply regret that we have to meet under these circumstances." Nic turns his attention to me. His posture stiffens, eyes narrowing with each step he takes. I lower my head, focusing on my feet. My mouth dries, and I swallow the phantom spit as the older man, my guardian, looms over me.

"Ceres," I flinch as he utters my name with a deep, measured tone. "What happened?"

Wincing, I fix my gaze on the floor, my jaw tensing. "Ceres?" I shift my glare to the wall.

"Idiot jocks got what they deserved. Now they're crying to their mummies." Nic exhales a weary sigh.

"I hoped we were beyond such incidents by now." I stay silent. Nic turns away; I glimpse him, shaking his head in disappointment. "I apologise for the turmoil she has caused. Whatever expenses Medicare doesn't cover, I will gladly compensate," he declares to the families.

"That's insufficient," one mother retorts sharply. "My son is traumatised! You must expel her!" I raise an eyebrow at her exaggerated outrage.

"Sure, traumatised. If the monkey is smart enough to be emotionally damaged." Nic whirls back to me, his eyes ablaze.

"Ceres!" I flinch as my name reverberates off the office walls. I slump further, staring down at the stained teal carpet. "I expected better from you."

The families all fidget nervously, their eyes darting between the door and me, as if they are calculating their escape route should they need to flee. Their hearts palpitate faster, the thick scent of fear permeating the air.

Zack observes silently, his jaw set firmly. I can see the unspoken protest in his eyes. He's poised to defend me, but we both understand the futility of it.

"The hospital bills will follow," the mother states, her voice quivering as she quickly guides her son out the door. The others hastily follow suit.

Nic's shoulders droop as he releases a heavy breath before addressing the principal.

"I'll ensure my company makes an additional contribution," Nic concludes. The principal's face tightens, resembling one who has just tasted something bitter.

"You assured me to there would be no more incidents." Nic's jaw sets firmly. "However, the school could benefit from a new assembly hall, one sizeable enough for the Sunday mass," he proposes. Nic casts the man a stern look before conceding.

"Fine. Send me the estimates, and we'll sponsor the new facility." Nic then fixes his gaze on Zack, scrutinizing the young man. "What was your involvement in all this?" he demands. Zack's mother remains unresponsive, staring blankly, lost in a drug infused haze. I'm amazed she managed to drive here at all.

"He was merely caught in the crossfire. I instigated the fight." Nic and Zack's eyes lock in a silent battle, a fierce animosity simmering between them that could ignite the room.

"Let's go, Ceres," Nic commands, striding towards the door. I cast Zack one last glance before trailing after Nic.

Nic unlocks the car and gets in. He peers through the window, expecting me to follow suit. I notice the disappointment etched on his face. Resigned, I toss my bag in and slump into the seat, slamming the car door shut. Nic's lips press into a thin line, his hand grips the steering wheel and crushes the button, locking the car, and starts the engine.

"What were you thinking?" he demands, barely containing his frustration.

"I don't want to talk about it."

"When do you ever?" My body tenses, my gaze fixed intently on the windscreen. "You've neglected your studies. You refuse to communicate with me. You can't just start fights like a child, you need to grow up and start acting like an adult." I maintain my silence, the bitter guilt bubbling to the surface. Nic pauses, awaiting a response, but he knows my tendency for silence in such moments. "Honestly, Ceres. You had made such progress, no altercations in over a year! If it wasn't for that miscreant."

"Zack is not to blame," my voice fails me. Nic draws a deep breath before continuing.

"You isolate yourself, refusing to socialise with anyone. I'm worried about you. I want what's best for you." A sharp stab hits my chest.

"I had one friend."

"He was a negative influence on you. I'm relieved he's no longer in the picture. He hurt you, clearly expressed his desire to distance himself. Why persist in a friendship with someone so harmful?"

A memory resurfaces vividly.

"I don't want to see you again," Zack grits, avoiding eye contact, his fingers curled tightly, knuckles turning white with tension. The room darkened as clouds obscured the sun, his figure rigid like a statue, the visible tension and anger threatening to shatter his composure. "Your friendship is suffocating."

It was clear as if it were yesterday. We both experienced pain and grief, a friendship we believed could withstand any storm. It shouldn't have shaken me so profoundly. Our arguments became more frequent, our time together less enjoyable, until we could barely stand each other. I close my eyes and draw a deep breath. Why did I flee that day? Why didn't I attempt to reconcile?

I remain silent, aware of the futility of arguing. Regardless of my feelings, Nic always has a counterargument.

'Your feelings are wrong. Stop acting like a child.' Nic's words echo in my mind, replacing the bitter guilt with resentment.

I sit motionless in the seat, avoiding any interaction with my phone or making any noise. I withdraw further into myself, distancing as much as possible from Nic. His gaze flickers to the ceiling, a silent plea for patience in his eyes. "The school suggests you see a counsellor."

"I don't need one. Remember our agreement? I won't our waste time. I'll continue my training and attend high school." he nods in acknowledgment.

"I remember, but this incident is the last straw, Ceres. The destruction you've caused is unacceptable, and it reflects poorly on me. How do you think that looks?" I keep silent. "It's a poor reflection, Ceres, and it complicates matters when my profession is involved."

'You always cared about your reputation

more than me.'

Nic sighs once more and clears his throat. "You need to talk to someone. I've scheduled a session with the school counsellor. I believe he can provide the help you need. You'll meet Mr. Rose at ten am on Thursday." he glances briefly in my direction before returning his attention to the road.

"This is fucked,"

"Excuse me?" Nic's tone hardens. I avert my gaze, staring out the window. An internal rage simmers within me, urging me to lash out. I'm like a caged wild animal, desperate for release. "This is for your benefit. Please remember that." I inhale deeply, suppressing the brewing storm within.

"Fine."

"I'm doing this for your well-being," he repeats. I look away, and we drive home engulfed in silence.

Chapter 2

Year 2005

I raised my handheld console in the air, chasing the lights from the streets. I was desperate to illuminate the dark screen, eager to make progress in my game before we reached home.

Mum and Dad sat in the front seats of the car, conversing quietly. Complaints about our family flowed from their lips, concerns for Mum's older sister. Dad nodded in agreement but grumbled about Grandma and her self-absorption. This mattered little to me.

"Ceres," Mum called to me. "When we get home, change into your PJs so I can read you a story. Ok?"

"Ok," I reply.

"What the fuck!"

"Honey, look out."

The seat belt constricted around my waist and held tight across my chest as the car somersaulted across the empty road. My head bashed against the car door, and my body was tossed around like a rag doll.

The bangs and crunches of the car echoed in my ears before rolling to a final stop against a tree. Everything hurt. My vision blurred, fading in and out. Trembling, I reached for the belt with my hands. My voice failed me as I tried to call for my mum.

Chapter 3

Every morning I wake up to the searing image of my parents' lifeless bodies tangled in the wreckage of the car, as an unrelenting spectre in my mind. Even now, years later, I can recall the heat of the fiery blaze that consumed the car.

I can still see my mother, her head contorted in an unnatural angle, her once-kind eyes staring blankly into nothingness. The way her body seemed to fuse grotesquely with the twisted metal of the car, a horrific display of flesh and steel. My father, who always seemed invincible, lay broken and lifeless, his once-strong hands now limp and ashen. The smell of burning rubber and charred flesh assaults my senses, as if I were there again. My stomach churns at the memory.

This memory has haunted me since the accident, reliving the moment over and over in my sleep. Days melded into months, then years. I've grown to not fear the memory but to welcome it as an old friend, a cruel reminder of what I've lost.

I don't remember their voices or the warmth of their hugs, but the love they had for me lingers, a ghostly presence in my heart. That love, compared to Nicolai's iron rule and standoffish care, makes me prefer to chase the ghosts who loved me.

"Ceres! Get up, or you'll be late for the bus!" Nic voice echo's up to my room. A loud sigh escapes me as I resist leaving the soft comfort of my bed, my gaze fix on the white ceiling. No matter how brightly the sun shines, the world around me feels dim, lifeless.

"Up and at 'em, radioactive man," I mutter.

My room is a sanctuary of pop culture items from over the years, with not a single book in sight. A large TV faces my bed, sitting comfortably on a black shelf. My blue walls adorned with posters of the bands I admire, along with picture frames, hang just over my bed, capturing a selfie with me and my favourite bands. Short Stack, For Our Hero, and Heroes for Hire.

My pops sitting on the shelf, their black beady eyes watching me as I tease the ends of my brown chest nut short, spiked hair, adding a rebellious touch to my punk-inspired look.

My gaze drifts at the plastic statues, reminiscing about my childhood video games and anime. My hazel eyes shimmer with nostalgia. Pokebeasts, Empire Hearts, Spiro the Dragon, King of Games and All Piece, all displayed as a reminder to keep enjoying the things I love.

With a sigh, I observe the dull uniform I put on for five days a week. Wishing I could wear my usual attire, a singlet hanging from my shoulders, sitting over my lean frame. My hands buried in black skinny jeans with teared holes in them and a studded belt around my waist, holding my pants in place. But no, stuck wearing a formal white shirt and a horrid navy blue pleaded skirt. I hate uniforms.

Thumping down the stairs, I rush into the open-space kitchen, which melds together with the dining room. I pack my books and sort out my timetable for the day. Slipping my phone into my pocket, I hurry over to the vanilla-top kitchen and open the brown cupboard.

"Morning, Ceres!" the familiar voice greets.

"Morning, Nic," I respond, grabbing the kettle and filling it with water. Nic is already grabbing a reusable cup from the cupboard next to the white fridge and freezer. A gentle smile graces his thin lips as he watches me set the kettle on.

"Sleep well?" he brushes a strand of his blonde hair from his face and sipping his tea.

I shrug before answering, "Eh, same old, same old."

"The same dream?" His blue eyes gazing at me intently.

"Yep, nothing new." Pouring the boiling hot water into my cup and grabbing my school bag.

"What about breakfast!" Nic calls out as I approach the front door.

"I'm going to be late for the bus! See you when I get home!" I yell back, crossing the threshold and shutting the door behind me.

I hear Nic sigh and scrape the dining room chair legs over the vinyl floor. Digging into my pocket, I wrestle for my headphones, finally securing them and pressing play. Music fills my ears, making the world seem a little livelier, as if I'm part of a music video playing out the story the song has planned.

I gaze at the orange brick blocks of the high school as clouds loom over, darkening the sky. A flash of lightning strikes down the trees, bend and creaks against the wind. High school is every quirky kid's nightmare, every creative individual's dream killer. Academics are praised, jocks are heralded as heroes, and society looks down on creatives, musicians, and artists for not fitting into their system. Forced to be part of the machine, that doesn't make space for our unique cogs, they cut, pull apart, and shove us into their perfect working-class system until we die, keeping the government's pockets full. Is this truly living? Sitting behind a desk, working a nine-to-five job, surviving till the next paycheck? They only praise us for what we have, not for what we have lived. This society is suffocating, and people wonder why the youth considers death as a blessing.

As I take a step into this purgatory, I'm surrounded by the blind who follow orders without question, jumping off cliffs blindfolded, believing it'll save them. Cruel to anyone's individuality.

'Did you hear what she did?'

'Yeah, she took on a bunch of guys and beat them up.'

'Shouldn't she be suspended?'

Wherever I go in this school, students part like the Red Sea, all keeping their distance, the familiar sweet smell of fear lingering in the air. All because I broke some kid's nose in year eight, an arm in year nine and some ribs in year ten. They deserved it.

It's like this every day: go to school, hear the usual gossip, grab my books, and go to class, a monotonous cycle that never seems to end.

Day in and day out, the first up on the class schedule is cruelty. There should be a punishment for teachers torturing their students with the cruellest form of torture known to the human race. An abuse that humanity has to face daily and fear those who enjoy this form of suffering. Math, modern society's most effective torturing method to extract information from any foe. All you need is a textbook and a math teacher, and soon all their secrets will spill.

If you asked me a simple addition or subtraction question and told me to answer it without a calculator, my brain goes offline.

I sit in the corner of the classroom, everyone in their own little cliques, far away from me. They're all laughing and talking, catching up from the weekend, talking about their cars. The boys bang their fists on the wooden desks, speaking about a girl. The plastic chairs bounce against the old brown carpet, laid upon the concrete slab since its construction. A slight ache worms itself into my chest. It would be nice to join in.

"Late again, I see, Mr. Castellan," Mr. Buckley's nasally voice breaks through the blaring noise of my headphones. My eyes trail over to the tall figure, their shoulders slouched, and a bandage covering his cheek.

He gives the teacher a sharp glare as he automatically beings playing with the black hanging skull on his left ear. "I believe you know the rules on piercings, Zack." Zack huffs and takes the skull out, grumbling under his breath. He walks over to an empty desk on the other side of the room, and Mr. Buckley continues the lesson, pausing between questions and asking students for answers. His eyes trail over to me. I continue to ignore the teacher and go at my pace, not caring to be part of the class, but, of course, Mr. Buckley has other plans. Walking over, he pulls out my headphone. "Care to be part of this class, Ceres?" Mr Buckley looks over my math book.

"To be honest, no." Mr. Buckley's eyes widen, not expecting the brutal honesty. He crosses his arms and puffs out his chest, steam seeming to come out of his ears. "You may be close to graduating, but you still have a test, and I expect you to cooperate." I only shrug my shoulders and put the headphone back in.

"I'm eighteen, sir. Technically, I could leave if I want to, considering I am a legal adult," I argue back and continue to write my math equations. All the idiotic boys cheer me on, and the girls laugh and whisper amongst themselves. I note Zack's smirk out of the corner of my eye.

"Then I hope you enjoy your time in detention," he walks back to his desk, writing out a paper slip. Sighing, I roll my eyes and pack my things. I take the paper from his hand as I leave the class and head to detention. At least I will find some peace there.

Halfway to the detention classroom, letting my subconscious consume my thoughts, my peers swiftly part from each other. Some move to the other side of the path or they wait for me to walk by. All of them give wide stares or giddy laughter and spread today's events like wildfire. I could easily let go, shut them up, give them something real to talk about. *'Is it worth it, Ceres?'* Nic's words whisper in the back of my head. Maybe. I stop walking, my consciousness swimming deeper and deeper into my darkest urges. A part of me wants to get rid of them, prove to all one way or another that I am not to be messed with. Clenching my fists, I feel the surge of rage coursing through my veins, their cruel voices in my head taunting me. Whispering wicked thoughts, telling me how easy it is to be rid of them, making it all look like an accident. It would be easy, wouldn't it? To be free of them all in one swift motion, but, of course, it will take a lot more than that to quell the anger deep inside.

Remembering the meditation Nic taught me, controlling this urge deep inside me. He and one other person are aware of this primal urge, aware of the dangers I hold. I am an odd human, something that concerns many other humans. They know something is off. Only prey can sense when a predator is among them.

I hold my books closer, gritting my jaw, and breathe.

Calming myself, I continue my journey to detention. I stay on the concrete path, passing the library, walking down the slopes to a little brick building known as block two. I trek up the staircase to the upper floor, standing before the dark green door.

"Back again, Ceres," Mrs. Bell sighs. All eyes in the room are trained on me. I nod in silence and pass the slip to her. Her talon-like nails grab the paper from my hands, her crow's feet eyes scan the paper, and she shuts her dull brown eyes as she inhales sharply through her crooked nose. "Take a seat. You can have one earbud while studying." I give a weak smile and nod, sitting in the corner of the room, opening all my books, and playing Short Stack on low. She shows sympathy toward students taught by Mr. Buckley.

Chapter 4

Dragging my feet through the door, I dump my schoolbag on the hooks with other assortments of belts, hats, jackets, and bags that have piled up over the years, forgotten. I extract my phone from my pocket and walk through the hall, mindlessly scrolling through social media.

"Hey! There she is!" I glance up from my phone to see Seth rising from the cream leather couch, arms wide, ready to envelop me in a hug. Seth is the type who behaves as though you've known each other forever after a few brief encounters. It's hard to forget his bright blue eyes and snow-white hair. He visits when work piles up, and he and Nic need to work overtime. Despite my curiosity, whenever I inquire about their job, they expertly change the subject. All I know is they work for a private government-contracted company called Hidebound, dealing in bio-research.

Seth wraps me in a hug, squeezing the air from my lungs before quickly releasing me.

He's affectionate and warms up to strangers quickly, reminding me of an overgrown, enthusiastic puppy. But he always carries an off-putting scent, a mix of something bitter and foul.

"It's, uh, good to see you," I start breathing through my mouth to avoid the smell of dog.

"Almost graduating. Are you excited?" An eager smile grows on his lips. I don't trust overly cheerful people.

"Yeah, I'll be glad to leave that hellhole," I shrug awkwardly shifting my weight from foot to foot.

Seth laughs and lightly taps me on the shoulder. "I bet you are!"

"As much as I'd love for you two to catch up, Seth, we need to focus!" Nic interrupts. I silently thank him, and Seth promptly returns his attention to their work. "Can you make your own dinner tonight?" Nic asks.

"I mean, I could, but should I? I had a long day at school, a very emotional day." I make my voice quiver as if on the verge of tears. Nic has seen through this act before. "Maybe, just maybe, we could have pizza tonight–cause today was so tough, ya know." I prolong the dramatics with fake sobs.

I peer through my fingers and smile when Nic rolls his eyes and chuckles. "I'll order us pizza."

"Pizza!" Seth exclaims from the other room.

"Best night ever!" I cheer, raising my arms.

"Order it online, and I'll give you my card!" Nic calls.

Giddily, I dart into my room, grab my laptop, and quickly order pizza for dinner. Food is my only motivator. Sure, there's more to life than food, but sometimes it's the small things that count.

"The pizza will be here in thirty!" I announce, leaning out of my room. I hear loud thumps as Nic ascends the staircase, a smile on his face as he approaches.

"Thank you. Card, please," he requests, extending his hand. I hand over the plastic rectangle reluctantly. "We don't want a repeat of last time," he reminds me, pocketing the card.

"I didn't hear complaints about the nice food I ordered," I retort.

"Yes, but not at my expense. Once you have a job, you can buy all the lovely food you want," Nic sighs, his shoulders slumping. "Which reminds me, I need to talk to you about something." Dread creeps up my spine, and my stomach plummets. Nic raises his hands in a calming gesture. "It's nothing bad. I'm just concerned about your future." I exhale the breath I'd been holding.

"Instead of suspense, why not tell me now?" Stepping down the stairs. Nic follows me to the lounge room.

I sit on the couch, arms crossed. Nic settles across from me, and Seth hesitates at the doorway. Nic begins, "I spoke with my boss about a position for you after high school." My body freezes, heart racing, a chill spreading through me. "They said yes." Panic sets in. I don't want this. I chant internally, fear clawing at my mind. "It's a great opportunity. You'd be mad to pass it up. Good pay, valuable skills." I swallow hard, fighting back tears. Do I even have a choice? "You can start as soon as the holidays begin. You're going to love it!" he concludes, optimism in his voice. Before I can respond, a loud knock echoes. Seth dashes to answer it. Nic gently touches my shoulder. "It'll be good for you. I'm worried about your future," he repeats before leaving to collect the pizzas.

I rise stiffly and retreat upstairs to my room. Leaning against the door, I slide to the floor, tears streaming down my face.

Chapter 5

Year 2005

"Ceres hasn't been socialising with the other children since arriving at this school." I overhear my teacher speaking from inside the classroom. "Do you know how she fared in her previous school? Did she struggle to make friends?"

"Not that I am aware, unfortunately," Nic replies. "After her parents' tragic deaths, she came into my care." I tense at the memory of their bodies twisted, fused with the wreckage. Their lifeless eyes haunting me.

"I see. What about her extended family? Have they been in contact with her?"

"No. Her family disowned her." I hadn't seen them since that horrific night.

"Has she maintained any friendships?"

"Only one, but he chose to distance himself." A lie.

"Oh. That is unfortunate," she sighs. "Mr. Treacher, I am concerned about her. Her

grades are slipping, and she is isolating herself. Are you providing adequate care?"

"I am. She is attending therapy." *Another lie. "And I believed enrolling her in self-defence classes would be beneficial."*

"What purpose does that serve?" her voice hardens.

"It offers numerous benefits: breathing techniques, anger management, and a chance to socialise. I assure you, she is making friends in the class." Another lie. No one there wishes to associate with me, either.

"I see," she replies tersely. "Please understand, if I don't see improvement, I will have to inform the authorities. Agreed?" I hear Nic's heart skip.

"Of course. I want what's best for her. I want her to thrive and connect with others." Yet another lie. Nic's instruction rings in my head: Never reveal what happens at home. People don't need to know our issues.

Both Nic and my teacher exit the classroom together. Nic flashes a radiant smile at me. Following Nic's instructions, I summon the strength to smile back.

"Ready to go home?" he asks. I nod and bid the teacher farewell.

A week later, she vanished. Never to be seen again.

Chapter 6

A groan echoes from the stairwell, accompanied by two heavy thumps, each followed by a brief pause. The sounds grow closer to the kitchen doorway. I retrieve another mug from the cupboard and spoon instant coffee into the bottom, then fill it with hot water from the kettle and grab milk from the fridge.

"Another late night?" Nic stands in the doorway, slouching against the wall, eyes lidded, dark bags weighing down his sockets. He shuffles closer to the counter step by step and takes the mug. After a sip, he heaves a deep sigh.

"Thank you," he murmurs, taking another sip. I simply shrug in response and return the milk, sipping from my fire-breathing dragon mug. "Seth and I were working on a project until late last night after you went to bed."

"I know. You came home around one this morning." Nic frowns into his coffee as if it disappoints him.

"What were you doing up at one in the morning?" I smile into my cup.

"Reading fan fiction," I laugh. "I was deep into this scene where two of my favourite band members were—"

"I don't want to know!" Nic cuts in, running out of the kitchen. My laughter fills the room, the perfect start to my day.

With my coffee finished and my bag over my shoulder, I bid a slightly traumatised Nic farewell and head for the front door.

How many weeks left until school ends—three, two, maybe four? Time has been inconsistent in my mind, my focus solely on surviving day by day, hoping to escape this perpetual hell hole. I wonder if leaving high school will rid me of this horrible ache in my chest or if it will continue consuming me.

Upon graduation, my desire is to escape this town, leave my past behind, and start anew in the city. Yet, Nic's words echo in my head,

'I've asked my boss if you can start after graduation.' My throat tightens. No thanks, I want to find *my* path in life, not be chained to a corporate job with its myriad rules, expectations, and backstabbers waiting for any chance to climb the ladder. My spirit is too free for such constraints.

As I traverse the school grounds, sadness and rage mix with my uncaring and hollow nature, turning into a corrosive acid that strips away my armour. I feel exposed, my raw and potent emotions laid bare. After more than a year of keeping my husk, feeling anything again is terrifying. I want nothing more than to hide from the prying eyes and cruel whispers. Today, I'm not equipped to deal with humanity.

'Mr Rose will be waiting for you at the library. Don't be late!' The message sears into my mind, igniting a seething hatred.

The loud chime of the bronze bell rings through the school's PA system. Life erupts as students flee their classrooms, laughing and rushing to their bags. Some shove books inside haphazardly, others rummage for their food, eager to claim the best spots under the shade, away from the sun's harsh rays.

I've grown accustomed to the isolation, finding solace in the library where I pretend to study but really watch anime, '*studying*' serving as the perfect guise.

"Ah, Ceres, do you need the computer today?" Mrs. Crow asks, her pale blue eyes looking down at me with an air of superiority that makes her unpopular among students.

"No, not today, thank you, Miss." She nods and turns her attention back to her monitor. Free from her gaze, I wander to the back of the library, meandering through the maze of bookcases. The familiar scent of books, snug side by side with an impressive layer of dust on top, fills the air. I ponder if they ever grow jealous, spending decades in the same spot, watching students pass by, forgotten through the ages.

A sense of unease grows within me, a pit forming in my stomach as the ache in my chest deepens, spreading like poison through my veins. We are like these books, easily overlooked, our graves collecting weeds and eroding under harsh elements, just as the masses ignore these books. Throughout history, only the greats are remembered.

I drew my attention to a lone door at the back of the library, its ominous and foreboding presence stark against the dull green doors I've passed. Made of oak with an old brass knob, it seems to beckon me closer, a welcoming presence that I know deep down is a trick. Would any average person be fooled, or would they sense the danger I feel?

With a deep breath, I grasp the cold brass knob and slowly turn. The door creaks open, revealing a dark empty room with a single light hanging above and grey concrete floor. A tall, lone figure stands in the centre, under the light and their mouth agape, green eyes fixed on me with a mournful expression. The door slams shut behind me, startling me from my daze, and I question how I moved into the dark room without a single step.

"You must be Ceres," the white-haired stranger says with a sad smile. "Thought you could skip out on our session?" they chuckle, moving closer. "I'm Luca," they introduce themselves. "Your counsellor." Brushing off the noticeable lint on their skirt, their muscled figure strains slightly against their white blouse, and my mind goes blank.

Chapter 7

"Wait, wait, wait," I shake my hands and head, my brain rebooting, words tumbling out incoherently. "What are you? What's happening? How did you…?" They gently place a finger on my lips, silencing me.

"This therapy helps my patients. I create a special room within an empty space – consider it a pocket dimension – and it makes them feel more comfortable, a place for them to feel safe. People are likelier to talk," Luca shrugs, breaking my spiral of thoughts. "When you touch the door, the room changes. The magic reacts strongly to other supernaturals, violently altering the room to their happy place." My eyes widen in disbelief. Luca surveys the dark room, their eyes glinting at the light above and then back to me. "Usually, it's something small with humans, like a video game or a childhood toy. Supernaturals prefer the beach, the forests, places they visited as children, but not you." Luca stops and looks around the empty space. My head falls into my palms, a loud groan escaping me as pressure builds in my skull.

"Great, I've officially lost it," I reply sarcastically.

"Hey, it's okay, you're not losing your mind," they assure me. I shake my head in denial.

"Nope, nope, nope," I interject. "How can you claim this is real? Magic, actual magic? Am I the only one oblivious to this?"

"No, the rest of humanity is unaware, with few exceptions, but I assumed you knew."

"No. You've blindsided me." The room trembles and the floor cracks and crumbles into the void. I glance at Luca, feeling a dull ache in my jaw. Luca's expression softens, their shoulders sagging slightly.

"I'm sorry," I cover my face with my hands and exhale loudly.

"Am I hallucinating? This can't be real." Luca chuckles lightly.

"Well, I am what you'd call a Magiq. Simply put." I shake my head in disbelief.

"Can we stick to plain English, please? I'm not following," I insist, locking eyes with them.

"A Magiq is a neutral term for witches and warlocks," they grimace.

"Fantastic. Now, why am I here?" I demand, the room quivering, the concrete floor cracking and crumbling at the edges.

"You're here because your guardian arranged a therapy session for you."

"And they neglected to mention you're magical."

"Technically, I'm standing in for Mr. Rose. He fell ill, and I replaced him." They give a nervous chuckle.

"That's hard to believe. You can't just appear because someone's mysteriously ill and then—poof!"

Luca steps back, putting distance between us. "I understand this seems suspicious, but I assure you, I'm here with the best intentions."

"Sure," I scoff.

"I know this is overwhelming, and I just shattered your perception of reality, but I mean what I said."

We fall into a long silence. Luca shakes their head and claps their hands together. "Let's talk." I swallow the growing lump in my throat, feeling it constrict with each passing moment. This room dark, barren with a single light hanging above, a cruel reminder of what has stripped away from me. A darkness eating me from the inside and what remains is a husk.

"Isn't it exhausting listening to all these problems?" I try to divert the conversation. The ground beneath my feet begins to reconstruct itself.

"Sometimes, but it helps people to know they have someone who will listen," they smile.

"That's good to know." The room returns to its original state, but I remain enveloped in a dark void.

"So, how do I change this room?" Luca frowns, surveying the area.

"It usually transforms into someone's happy place," they respond with a hint of sadness.

Silence envelops me as I delve into my inner thoughts, reflecting on years of emotion.

"Do I really have no happy memory?" Hoping for a reaction from the room. "Not even a small one?" Luca watches me expectantly, willing the room to transform.

"This room perfectly encapsulates everything," I concede with a shake of my head. "Sometimes I feel numb, hollow. Life has become a series of motions with no joy." I confess, finally releasing the pent-up emotions. Luca nods in understanding.

"Did you ever dream of anything as a child? How long have you felt this way?" I shrug, focusing on a distant corner.

"All I remember is my life veering off course eight years ago." I fight back tears, refusing to break down in front of a stranger. "Then I began to change. I could hear things from afar. Smells would overwhelm me to the point of nausea. I envied kids who got sick days; I never fell ill, not even food poisoning affected me."

"You envied them that much?"

"I didn't want to attend school… Zack wasn't there," I give a weak smile, recalling my protests at attending a different school with my best friend. "He only attended mine because he begged his mother after I refused, and then… he stopped wanting me around." My throat tightens further, the threat of tears imminent. "One day, he just stopped visiting. At school, he distanced himself, brushing me off, until finally, he said he didn't want me around anymore." My voice cracks, and I cough to clear it. Luca's expression shifts to concern, their hand reaching towards my shoulder. I step back, maintaining a distance. "I don't need pity."

Luca sighs and lowers their hand. "I'm not pitying you. I'm offering comfort." I clench my jaw and shake my head dismissively.

"We go to school, learn to survive in the rat race, graduate, work in underpaying jobs or accrue debt in university. The only escape from debt is a soulless corporate job with endless hours, and that's considered living!" Luca's expression softens.

"You have a choice. You're not bound to this path." It feels like a punch to the gut.

"A choice, you say? I've never heard that before."

"Not even from your guardian?"

"It's always *'you must go to training, to school, sign up for the corporation; it'll be great. You must see a therapist, stay away from that boy.'* It's constantly *'you must.'* And never *'what do you want to do?' 'Do you want to see someone?' 'Why is he important?' 'Do you want to take up kendo and kickboxing or prefer another hobby?'"* I can see the anger building in Luca's eyes. They take a deep breath, their fingers flexing. "I've never had a choice."

"What do you want?"

"I don't know." The room trembling around us. "I don't know what I want, what to do. I'm so tired," my voice cracks, "Tired of this life, this constant tedium. What's the point? I'm tired of conforming to the rules." As the room grows dark, only a single stream of light highlights Luca and me. The emptiness in my chest grows, feeling ready to implode. The lump in my throat remains, and tears threaten to spill.

Luca abruptly stands, eyes wide with fear, intently watching me.

"Ceres."

"I'm okay." The room stays dark. I take a deep breath, pushing down my emotions. My chest loosens, the tears recede, and my throat relaxes. I'm numb again.

"You shouldn't suppress your feelings," Luca pleads. "You need to express them, not bury them."

"What's the point? No matter who I tell, nothing changes." I offer a sad smile and turn away, leaving them in the dim room.

Chapter 8

Year 2005

In the centre of the room, a young girl with long, ringlet brown hair sat on a large leather couch, clutching her teddy bear tightly. Tears streamed down her face, and her eyes were puffy and red. As the office door opened, the young girl jumped, her head swiftly turning to the two gentlemen entering. Nic stood before the young girl, his appearance free from the wear of crow's feet or dark bags under his eyes, his hair vibrant and lush.

"Ceres?" the younger man approached the girl. His voice was gentle and warm, and she nodded, sniffling.

"I'm Nicolai. I'm going to be taking care of you."

"I want my mommy," she sniffled.

Nicolai nodded his head, swallowing the pain down his throat. "I know. I'm sorry, I really am."

Her chest grew tight, and tears threatened to spill from her eyes.

"Do you have to go?" Zack whimpered, wiping the stray tear from his watering eyes. As school children and parents left the grounds, Nic kept his distance, observing the situation, and Zack's mother did the same, her hands on her chest, feeling a dull ache as she watched her son throw his arms around his best friend.

"I have to. Nic says I have to," tears began to flow down her face. "But I can visit you, and we can hang out still," she says, sounding hopeful. Nic stepped in, keeping his distance from the sobbing children.

"I can't guarantee that you can, but I can try." Zack stepped in front of Ceres.

"And why not!?" Zack shouted at Nic.

"Zack!" his mother scolded him, but the boy kept going.

"You can't just take her out of the school, away from her friends!" he glowered, balling his fist, ready to take on the grown man.

"I am so sorry," Zack's mother stormed in and dragged Zack away from Nic.

"It's all right, I can understand. It's tough to say goodbye." Nic brushed the apology away and knelt down at Zack's eye level. "We'll make a day soon. Deal?" he asks Zack, but the boy ignored the man and hid behind his mother. Ceres heard Zack's mother apologise once more.

Year 2006

Zack barged into her room and plopped himself on her bed. His eyes sparkled with wonderment as he looked up at the glow-in-the-dark star stickers.

"Your new room is so much bigger!" his head turning to the corner of her room, his eyes lighting up at the bamboo swords and white uniform. Zack got up, hopped off the bed, and ran to the far end, picking up the sword. He gave Ceres a broad smile, but it disappeared when he saw the sullen face looking back at

him. "You don't like it?" she shrugged in response and sat on the bed.

"Nicolai thinks it would be good for me. I don't want to do it."

"But you get to use a cool sword!" She shrugged once more.

"Cool sword, using my fists to fight... but none of it will bring my parents back." Zack put the sword down and walked back to the bed, sitting beside her. His lips pursed, and his face screwed tight before gently hugging her.

"I don't know what it's like, but I know I would be really sad if I lost you," he holds her tight. Ceres gave a weak smile and hugged back, tears slowly trailing down her cheeks.

Year 2006

Ceres watches from the car, seeing Zack hiding behind his mother, and Nic talking to her in the driveway of her house.

"Are you sure? Ceres loves her consoles," she questioned Nic. Younger Ceres sat in the car, watching in dismay.

"Positive. I can't let Ceres play any violent games; I'm worried it may... trigger her," Nic whispered the last part, but no matter how quiet he was, Ceres could hear him. Everything had happened so fast when her parents died. Her hearing, her taste, her agility and strength. Something in her was changing. But this, her games, her saves, her progress, none of it was triggering.

"Oh god," Zack's mother murmurs, her eyes looking to Ceres in the car. "Is there anything I can do? I've known Ceres much longer; if she needs a familiar place to stay, we can-."

"It's not necessary," Nic interjected. Zack glared at Nicolai as soon as the man rejected his mother's offer. "What Ceres needs is a routine and I will be starting therapy shortly after." Zack's mother hesitantly but slowly nodded in agreement.

"Are you sure Ceres can't keep one?" Zack's mother gives Nic the handheld console back, but Nic refused.

"*I was going to donate them, but she insisted her friend to have them, so please, enjoy them.*" *with that last word, Nic turned on his heel and got into the car. He turned the ignition, and as the engine roared to life, Nic slowly reversed out of the driveway. Ceres gave a slow wave to Zack and watched them disappear from view.*

"*This will be good for you,*" *Nic interjected, breaking the silence between them.* "*Video games can be quite violent, and I'm worried about your nightmares.*" *Ceres remained silent on the matter, feeling her heart sink. She didn't think that was the case.*

Year 2012

"*I really want to go to TAFE and learn how the industry works, and I can learn how to manage venues!*" *her younger self exclaimed. Nic grimaced, his mouth turning downward more and more with each word leaving her mouth. The older man visibly sighed and turned to her.*

"And how are you going to get an income?" Ceres opened her mouth to reply but was quickly cut short. "I think it's best if you find another career or something to put food on the table. It's great you have all these dreams, but don't you think it's ... just a tad risky?" his voice increased with a higher inflection.

Ceres looked at him blankly. "But I want to do this course." Ceres tilts her head down and Nic's expression didn't change.

"If you do this course, you know you will have to take up extra training. You know that." Her eyes lit up, and she bobbed her head up and down.

"I don't get it. It's just some dead-end pipedream; it will never give her security. How will she ever buy a place with little money?" she heard Nic say. Her face fell, tears slowly building up. "I just wish she was more interested in academics and not this artsy crap."

"Look, I get you're frustrated, but just let the kid be a kid. It won't hurt," Seth reasoned.

"She's almost seventeen. It's going to be her last year soon; We're almost in the clear." Nic heaved a frustrated sigh.

"I know, I know."

Year 2012

She sat on the chair, and Nic was sitting next to her.

"I truly believe Ceres will benefit from this," the counsellor urges. Nic shook his head.

"No. I'm sorry, but Ceres' key priority is her training and her education. She doesn't need this extra activity," Nic argued. Helplessly, she looked defeated at the counsellor, knowing that once Nic made up his mind, he would not budge.

"Please, Mr. Treacher, I insist you think of Ceres' well-being! She is unhappy with training-."

"What?!" the counsellor jolted in her seat.

"Mr. Treacher, I will not tolerate this behaviour in my office. Speak like that to me

again, and I will report you." Nic steeled his gaze, fists clenched tightly.

"Very well. I will consider your words. Good day," Nic gritted and rose from his seat. Ceres gave the counsellor a sad but knowing smile and followed Nic shortly after. Once out of earshot and into the hallway, Nic turned to her. "You will not be seeing her again. Filling your head with foolish ideas, your training is important." Ceres gritted her jaw, tears slowly falling from her eyes.

"But I want to. I want to go, I want to learn about music, I want to try other things, Nic," her lips trembled. Nics gaze softened. Turning to the sixteen-year-old, he gently put his hand on her shoulder.

"Look, I understand. I really do, but your training, it's important. These violent outbursts with your peers, getting into fights. I only say this because I care about you."

"Can't I try both?" she sniffled. Nic pursed his lips, remaining silent for a few seconds.

"If you can find the time, then yes, you can try both," he agrees. She gave a weak smile in return. But she knew it never happened; lessons piled on, one after another, insisting she needed more time to learn restraint.

Chapter 9

'I receive a call from Mr. Rose. You haven't attended your session today. I will pick you up after training.' My brow furrows. Thumbs typing in quick succession.

'I did attend. What are you talking about? I was told he was ill and had a replacement.'

I am met with silence. Either Nic isn't having any of it or work has gotten in his way. My shoulders sag as I read the text over and over, my mind trying to make sense of the situation. I'll be receiving another lecture, regardless.

I look down at the empty tracks, patiently waiting for the train to arrive. Both headphones blare, blocking out the ruckus from kids in other schools.

All are roughhousing and throwing slurs at one another. Some have turned it into a war against other schools in the area. It's sad to say the private school I attend, despite being the best out of the bad bunch, is still pretty bad. If

I were to paint a picture of the area I live in, I could say we are the butt of the joke between the Gold Coast and Brisbane city, the bogans from Logan. I wish I could say I am lying, but I am not. It rhymes so well it makes sense why most of our crime is committed: car theft, dole bludgers, stabbings, drugs, and youth who aren't interested in seeking higher education, dropping out at year ten to get a contracting job. People would be offended, but I am only stating the truth. This is what Logan is like, but not all the time. Only in certain areas, and some of Logan can be nice. Plus, we even make fun of ourselves. Those who do not live in the area do not have that privilege; only we have that right as we live in it day by day. I am a bogan from Logan, but only I can call myself that.

I would also be lying if I said I wanted to stay here in the area where nothing seems to be going forward. I feel so trapped and restricted; I yearn to know what happens in city life.

Feeling like everything is happening, something is always going on, and I can't see it.

Nic's words only echo in my head. *'The city? You know there are plenty of dojos nearby, right?'* I smile to myself. I do, but I need something to get me out of here.

The train signals its arrival, the horn blasting as it slows upon arrival.

Why am I even doing this? The question echoes in my mind as I deflect the punch with ease. Exhaustion from training weighs heavily, both in body and mind. Dodging my opponent's grip, I seize their wrist in a swift, determined motion. I don't want to do this relentless training, this all feels meaningless.

I grip tighter around the fragile bone, feeling the dense calcium crack in my hand. A piercing scream breaks me from my thoughts.

"You're a bloody psycho!" my opponent screams, cradling his wrist. I look at my hand, remembering how it felt, the bone breaking, slowly cracking like an eggshell. It was so easy. If I applied more pressure, the bone would have snapped. a shiver trails down my spine and a sickening desire grew within my chest, I want to break the bone, hear him scream once more.

"Ceres." Sensei snaps, rushing over to the student and assessing his wrist. "Sit this one out." Hamish takes a step back from me, clinging to his wrist, staring at me with an intense gaze. I keep my eyes on him, feeling a rumble rise in my throat, my fingers itch, ready to grab hold and hear the screams once more. "Ceres!" Sensei's voice is more forceful this time, redirecting my attention. He gestures towards the wall furthest from everyone. "Go and cool off. The rest of you, back to training!"

Trudging towards the wall, I feel every gaze in the dojo. My steps burden with confusion. Where did this desire come from? Why did I lose control? These unanswered questions swirl in my head.

Standing against the wall, I focus on regulating my breath, closing my eyes. I concentrate on each inhale and exhale. I was so close to losing myself to this desire, it was as if a beast had woken within, snapping its teeth, wanting to tear into flesh. What is wrong with me?

The sounds of training continue behind me – the impact of fists and feet, the grunts of exertion – but they feel distant, as if I'm separated from the rest by an unseen barrier.

With another deep breath, I turn to the face the group, watching, waiting till I am allowed to join once more.

The clock hits nine as we finish for class. The two groups split into the changing rooms. Getting ready to venture out into the night, they check their phones and double-check timetables so they can catch the bus or train on time. I can understand the fear of not wanting to be alone late at night. I can appreciate getting home safely as their top priority. You don't know who lurks in the shadows, waiting for a lone soul to pass them by, patiently waiting till they finally strike. Opportunity is the keyword. They never attack unless the opportunity presents itself. That is the cruel reality of this world.

"Oi, Ceres, you on crack or something? You nearly snapped that guy's wrist," Lea, a fellow peer of mine here at the dojo and her posse of followers back her. I roll my eyes at the girl, used to her remarks. I pack my stuff and continue to ignore her. "God, you're pathetic. You should have died with your parents." I slam the locker door shut. The metal clashing against metal, the sound resonates within the room. Jolting the mousy girl from her fragile façade. My eyes land on the girl, their breath hitching in their throat. All take a step back and tremble from my gaze.

"Want to say that again?" I hiss, and an unexpected growl resonates through my chest, storming closer to the young woman, fists clenched, ready to strike. She scrambles backwards, and her friends flee. She is alone.

"I-I-I," she stutters, shrinking back even further. The growl rises up my throat. I hold back the urge to lash out, remembering sensei's words. 'You use these skills for self-defence, not to fight.' I wanna do more than just punch her stupid northsider face. Lea takes my restraint as her chance and flees, stumbling over her feet, nearly hitting the floor again before finally reaching the door. I bare my teeth where she once stood and let out a snarl.

"This is why I don't like hanging around humans," I mumble to myself. After witnessing my threatening gaze, all the girls quickly depart, all scrambling to get away and not be in the firing line. I wouldn't have done anything to them unless I was provoked. I can still feel the burning rage deep inside me, the adrenaline kicking in. Shoving the rage down, I grab my bag, the last one to leave the dojo, and wait for Nic to come and get me. *You don't pick me up unless you want to talk!*

I was never afraid of the dark, nor did I fear what others feared. I knew I could hold my own. I always felt peace as night fell, able to calm and recollect my thoughts. I would even feel small when looking up to see the stars. Though I cannot see them now, I know they are there. I sometimes ask the universe to throw me a bone, give me a sign, a purpose. I feel so lost in this world, like I am just existing, stumbling through life as I try to find my way. I just need something. Nic's car pulls up when I ask for the sign. I only sigh to myself and look back up at the night sky. This is not the sign I am asking for!

"So… good lesson?" Nic asks me. I shrug and pull out my phone, going through my notifications. Nothing from social media but plenty coming from all the video game apps I've installed, money-hungry thieving apps.

"Your instructor called me, mentioned how you nearly broke someone's wrist." I tighten my lips and glare at the screen.

"At least they didn't mention the locker room." My mind drifting back to the moment, reflecting the dark desire to inflict pain, to bare my teeth and smile. It's not the first time I've felt this way.

"What happened in the locker room?!" I remain silent.

Chapter 10

Same day, same routine, same everything. Wake up, get ready, go to school, eat, sleep, rinse and repeat. It's tedious. I ponder if this will be life. Instead of going to school, it'll be some job I despise, questioning my life's purpose. The more I dwell on it, the more trapped I feel. How do I escape?

Can I break free and forge my path, or am I stuck under his shadow? Always watching me, ensuring I follow the choices he has made for me.

'I'm doing this because I care about you.'

'I'm concerned about your future.'

'These dreams are great, but they won't sustain you.'

The pencil snaps in two. I stare at the sharp broken ends and sigh. Another pencil gone. That's twenty-three in one year.

"Ceres," I hear a deep voice call my name within the classroom. Everyone's eyes turn to me, the group of boys shouting, a small group of girls watching in silence, and others whispering amongst themselves. The principal stands at the door. "Could you come with me, please?"

It's not unusual for the principal to call for me, but this time I know I haven't done anything wrong. I follow the man back to his office and there stand two police officers. I look at them, a spike of fear in my chest.

"Have I done something wrong?" I ask out of reflex. The principal shakes his head.

"You're not in trouble," the principal assured me. "We just have some questions."

"Questions about what?" I ask, my anxiety mounting.

"You were close with Zack Castellan. Did he contact you before he disappeared?" one officer asks.

My world stops. "Disappeared?" my brain flatlines. The room spins, my stomach plummets, and a suffocating tightness grips my throat. Tears blur my vision as I struggle to breathe. The officers and the principal rush to my aid as I collapse to my knees.

"Ceres," their muffled voices call out to me.

Gone. The word echoes in my mind. Zack, gone? A torrent of emotions crashes over me. Betrayal, confusion, fear. I bombard them with questions. "When? How? Who saw him last?"

"He's been missing for four days. His mother was the last to see him after an argument," another officer explains.

I manage to speak through my tears. "We were friends, but he cut all contact a year ago."

I recount what I know–his troubled home life, his mother's problems, his reluctance to go home. The officers continue their questioning, but their words fade into a blur as I struggle to process the shock.

"I need to go home." my voice barely a whisper.

"Hey, the school just called, are you-." I push past Nic and race upstairs to my room. Nic calls my name. I ignore him and swing the door shut. The frame shakes from the force, the plaster cracks and wood on the door cracks. I grow more frustrated at the door, snarling at the piece of wood. I slam my fists against the door and it snaps in two. The door comes off its hinges, falling to the floor with a loud thump. I collapse on my knees and scream. Nic races up the stairs, bewildered at the sight.

Nic carefully and slowly moves closer, stepping over the broken pieces and gently reaching for me.

"Don't touch me," I snarl, feeling a dull ache in my upper jaw. Nic snatches his hand away and becomes rigid. His eyes widen, and fear settles in his bones. "He's gone!" Tears streaming like a waterfall at this point. Nic's shoulders fall, as does his mouth. He pales and continues to stare.

"You're not serious, are you?" I snap my eyes at the shaking man. They burn with rage as I look at him, shaking in his place.

"Why would you care?" You have your wish, considering you never liked him!"

I clench my jaw, the dull throb turning into an intense ache that radiates through my entire jawline. It feels like my teeth are shifting, elongating, morphing into something unfamiliar. Panic prickles at the edges of my mind as I run my tongue along the growing sharpness. Something is wrong. "We'll never see Zack again. He's gone." Rage subsides, and sadness takes over again. Tears keep flowing down my cheeks, and the dull ache in my jaw goes away.

"Ceres," Nic croaks.

"Don't! Don't bother. I just… I just want to be alone." Nic scrunches his face and has a mental argument. I can tell he wants to stay, but he also wants to respect my decision. Nic finally takes a step back and goes downstairs without a word.

I lie on the hardwood floor of my room and cry, tears falling onto the varnished wood.

This has to be a nightmare. Where would he go? Why did he leave? What pushed him?

Why couldn't he have said goodbye? Why didn't he tell me in the end? Did I really mean nothing to him?

I get up from the floor. My legs shake under my weight. I feel like a newborn deer learning to walk for the first time. I change out of my uniform, grabbing my casual bag, shoving my charger in and my phone into my pocket. Stomping downstairs, I make my way to the door.

"Where are you going?" Nic asks. I walk past and grab my shoes.

"Out." I watch Nic stiffen in his place, his eyes burning a hole in the side of my head.

"Where?" I resist the urge to sigh at the man.

"Don't know. Wherever the wind takes me."

"What - Ceres! What has gotten into you?" Nic surges forward. His calloused hands grab hold of my arm.

"I'm going to find Zack."

"What?"

"I said." Ripping my arm from Nic's hold. "I'm going to find Zack!"

"Even after what he did to you. After all the pain this boy caused you. You're foolish enough to go looking for him." I stop midway through the yard. Turning my gaze to the man, a burning frustration bubbling beneath my breast. Nic takes a step back.

"I'm pissed but." I swallow the lump forming in my throat. "He's the only friend I had, and I would be a fool if I gave up on him." Nic shouts my name as I walk away from the house, with a single destination in mind.

Chapter 11

Year 2011

Zack remained silent as we walked back to his house. His gaze was distant. I could tell he was reflecting and recounting the moments of this week. It was why I was here.

I could hear his heart beating rapidly. I grasped his hand, and his breath steadied.

He tightened his grip as we approached the old Queenslander home.

"Mum!" he called as we entered. Silence greeted us.

Zack grimaced and moved toward his mother's bedroom door, bracing for what awaited.

She lay on the bed, dishevelled, her mouth slack and open, drool dribbling from the side. He watched her intently, holding his breath as her chest rose slowly. He exhaled in relief when he saw the movement.

Zack headed to the kitchen and started searching through the cupboards. I joined him, recalling her usual hiding spots when she was on alcohol.

Back of the container cupboard, hiding in sealed containers, in the pantry at the back on the lowest level, behind poisons under the sink.

If not the kitchen, it would be the linen cupboard, the laundry buried under dirty clothes, her room, or somewhere in her workplace.

"Found it," his arm sticking out from the glasses cupboard, waving a box of opioids.

Zack crushed and flushed the white powder down the sink. If it weren't pills, it'd be vodka instead.

Ever since her head injury, she'd needed a vice. She became a different person, and Zack's life turned unstable.

Our routine whenever I visited had become predictable: check on his mother, find and destroy whatever substance she'd acquired, and prepare dinner.

"You skipped school the other day."

"Mum had an appointment, and I was the only one who could drive her." Zack nodded while peeling a potato.

I slammed the knife down on the broccoli with a loud bang against the board. "You've been skipping a lot because of her. I know you love her." Zack stopped peeling. "But you can't keep sacrificing yourself like this."

"And what! Leave her like Dad did!" he slammed the peeler down.

"You're not her parent." I heard Zack's heart skip a beat. His hands began to shake a little. "She's meant to care for you, not the other way around. You were forced to mature fast, get a job, a license, just to drive her everywhere. It isn't fair to you."

"I know," he whispered, peeling the potatoes once more with shaking hands. "But what can I do? No matter how many therapists she sees, antidepressants she takes, she chooses the pills or the bottle every time!"

"You can leave." Zack shot me an icy glare. "I know you resent your dad for leaving, but everyone has their limits. You've tried to help her, taking her to rehab, paying with your own money. But in the end, only she can save herself. She's not willing to do that, Zack, and it's okay to say enough is enough." Tears rolled down his cheeks. "Don't feel guilty. In the end, you need to think about your life, what you want from it, what you most want to do," I urged, my hands cradling his head.

"Why does she do this?" he croaked. "Why can't she fight for me?"

"Sometimes someone's demons are so strong they forget about the people who love them. It drowns out their love, tricking them into believing they are better off gone. I know you love her, but in the end, you have to protect yourself as well." Zack wrapped his arms around me, holding me close.

"I'm so tired. I don't want to do this anymore."

"I know."

Chapter 12

Walking closer, I see the house coming into view. The grass is dry and dead, the garden unkempt with only a few mother-in-law tongues growing in pots, the rest filled with dirt and dead plants. The house, your typical Queenslander, stands on all four stilts, combating the summer floods. Boards with weathered white paint are chipped and splintered by time. You need both arms to open the windows with frosted glass and hinged locks. The scorching sun has faded the wooden steps, each one creaking, the nails oxidised from the heat. The glossy finish of the green paint on the railings has worn off, only the carved gum leaves on the wood remaining. The veranda, enclosed with plastic sheets dangling from the tin roof, is a desperate effort to keep out rain and mosquitos. It isn't as spacious as it once was. The outdoor furniture has become discoloured, and the fabric has grown a layer of black mould. The veranda floor is littered with buckets, plastic shopping bags, boxes, broken chairs, and old toys. It's hard to get to the door because it's cluttered with shoes.

I stare at the old screen door, noting the holes left by the dog, Zack had so many years ago.

Taking a deep breath, I gently knock on the metal frame. The door rattles against the wood, loudly echoing down the dark hall. I hear footsteps within the house, rushing to get to the door. A figure approaches and stops midway down the hall. She slows her pace, her hand reaching for the metal knob, the crunch of the springs under pressure. The door swings open, and the familiar woman I once called my second mother stands before me.

Her eyes still weep, carrying the deep sorrow she feels for losing her only son. Her lips can't find the strength to form a smile when looking at me. She doesn't seem to be here, hiding in the depths of her mind, believing her son is only missing, and soon - one day, he will return.

She visibly swallows and opens her mouth.

"Ceres?" I nod gently, bracing for her reaction. She inhales deeply and moves out of the doorway. "Come in."

I take one step in, reminiscing about the times I came through this exact door. The old wood is no longer varnished with a smooth finish; it's patchy and scratched up. Throwing my shoes off at the door, I feel the rough floorboards against my feet. The air gushes through the cracks from the hollow space underneath.

Thundering down the halls, chasing each other to the only room that held the TV. Fighting over the controller; no one wanted to be player two. Afternoon tea, milo and fairy bread, eating and drinking as fast as we can just to get back to the game we played.

These walls are so thin, you can hear everything within the house. The heavy raindrops hitting the tin roof, feet walking on the floorboards, and the sound of children laughing from old cartoons. But then yelling - the kind you want to hide away from, pretending your family isn't falling apart.

"You know where his room is," Zack's mother grunts and skulks back to her own room, slamming her door shut. I jump at the sound, feeling the wind knock into me. What was once pain, is now replaced with burning frustration. How could she let herself become this? why wasn't she strong enough for Zack? How could she have done this to him?

The halls are littered with old magazines, books, and rubbish. The old living room is filled with lavish exercise machines and their boxes, bowls of half-eaten cereal and two-week-old milk sit in their glasses. They made a small trail amongst the junk to get to the television.

It makes sense why Zack insisted on coming over to mine. His mum changed so much since the divorce. I stare blankly at the black door, poorly painted, still able to see the old paint seep through. I grasp the old brass knob, turn it and push the door open.

Unlike the house, Zack's room is clean. The only piece he can keep in order amongst the destructive chaos. He covered all four walls in photos of the past, a bit of memory sealed away in one snapshot. Zack received a camera on his ninth birthday. It was a cheap disposable camera. I laugh to myself, thinking back - we had to take the film to get it developed at a chemist. The first photo he ever took is of me shoving a slice of chocolate cake into my mouth. It's the first photo you see when you walk in.

Gently closing the door behind me, I inspect the photos. Recognising the moments captured within them. Some are of Zack and me together, some landscapes across the bush and lush rainforests, and most of me. Either doing something monotonous, like homework, not even looking at the camera, and others pulling a silly face or giving him the bird. I snort and go over to the wall at the back of his room.

I look up, and the photos of me disappear; they are all scenery shots, of the mountains, lorikeets, some of the water dragons around school, the bin chickens fighting over scraps in the rubbish bin.

Kookaburras' heads are blurred because they are midway through whacking their prey to death before devouring it whole. I can see the legs of the small skink sticking out from its beak.

I look to the last wall, and there's only one photo. I walk closer, noticing the short hair, fringe dyed red, sitting by herself, eating a sandwich, and the sadness held deep within her own eyes. Me.

I gently grasp the photo off the wall. A deep ache grows within my chest, remembering the moments when this photo was taken. It was only a week after we parted ways. I remember crying myself to sleep, wanting to grasp the courage and snap him from this departure he had put between us. I wanted my best friend back - I want him back.

The painful lump remains in my throat, and the hole in my chest grows inside, allowing the ache to flow deeper into my veins. Threatening salty tears, only one eye leaks a single tear.

I take a deep breath, shuffling over to his bed and gently sitting on the spring mattress. It creaks under my weight; I bounce slightly, but come to a stop. Taking deep breaths, desperate to process this feeling beneath my breast. The sleepovers, homework discussions, daily problems, and birthdays all came to a stop. All of it.

I look up for what felt like an hour, noticing the chest of drawers opened. Clothes are gone from each level.

I look over to see his desk, the lone gift box sitting on top, his laptop and charger missing. A thin layer of dust sits on top of it all. Next to Zack's desk is a small metal trash bin. Scrunched-up balls of paper fill the bucket halfway. Two pieces pique my curiosity, moving my feet and getting up from the bed. The first is a small yellow note sticking to the side of the basket. An address scrawled neatly in cursive. Legible for any millennial to understand. An icy chill runs through my veins. It's a clue, a lead. Stuffing the paper in my pocket, I draw my attention to the white ball in the trash. My name is messily scrawled.

I unfurl the crinkled blue-lined white paper. Zack's words are heavily scratched out and rewritten, pen marks all over the paper, and ink splotches at the bottom, making the rest ineligible. In all the years I have known Zack, at least I can make out his handwriting.

> ~~'Dearest Ceres,~~
>
> ~~Happy 18th birthday, sorry I never wished you happy birthday before . . . I just . . . . had a lot going on.~~
>
> ~~Dear Ceres,~~
>
> ~~Happy 18th birthday. Hope your day is good.~~

Dear Ceres,

I'm sorry. I'm sorry about how things ended between us. I'm sorry I pulled away. I'm sorry for causing you so much pain. I had no choice. I could have lost you forever if I didn't step back.

Telling you the truth was something I wanted to do for so long, but my fear of losing you forever got in the way. I couldn't tell you right away. I had to wait.'

I stare at the letter blankly, my mind trying to make sense of the note. I look back to the black and red gift box. I gently remove the red ribbon and slowly lift the cardboard lid. Inside is my old handheld. The same indents on the left corner, the rubbed-out letters on the buttons, and the familiar red cartridge sitting on the back.

I flick the switch up, and the game comes to life. The same pixelated tone rings in my ears, and the familiar black and grey pixels battling it out on the opening screen. Pressing the button, I load the menu and there it is. My file, the same one I had since I was a little girl. The tears I held back break free, streaming down my cheeks. I click into the save, and there is my character, my progress, and my beloved Blazedrake. Still here, waiting for me to come back.

I jump from my thoughts as I hear a loud bang outside the room. Stuffing the handheld in my pocket, I creep out of his room and carefully walk down the hall.

I find Zack's mother back in the kitchen. Her eyes puffy red, boxes of empty pills scattered on the kitchen table. She sits on the wooden chair, like a mannequin in a store display. Lifeless eyes stare into the abyss. Her chest barely moves, and her skin is a waxy pale. I grasp her hands and kneel before her; she acknowledges me with a stare, just enough cognitive thinking to see who is in front of her.

"I need you to tell me everything. What happened before he disappeared?" I whisper. Zack's mother's throat bobs, and her eyes begin to water.

"We had a fight," her voice rough as sandpaper. Her eyes shift to the boxes on the table. "Angry at me. Told me I am a terrible mother," she grimaces. "He just grabbed his laptop and left." The dam breaks, and her tears fall.

I rise from my knees and take one last look at the kitchen. Zack's mother remains in her seat, her hands gripping together.

"I'll try to find him," I eave her alone once more.

The front door closes with a heavy clack. A heavy sadness weighs on my chest and feet as I take each step back down to the ground level.

Chapter 13

The bat cave. The only name scrawled on the crumpled note. I'm lucky to get results online, but nothing makes sense. It's just a cave. Why would Zack go into the cave?

The same caller ID appears again for the twenty-seventh time, followed by a barrage of text messages, each conveying an unfamiliar emotion ranging from anger and sadness to worry, pleading, and false promises.

I climb down the rocky terrain, following the sound of dull thumping beats, nearly tripping. Another call. I yank my phone out of my pocket and answer.

"What do you want, Nic?" I snap.

"Don't snap at me. Where are you? Why have you ignored my calls? You've missed training!"

"I'm searching for Zack,"

"Are you serious? Ignoring all your responsibilities for some boy!"

"He's not just 'some boy'! He's my friend, a friend who's missing."

"Friend? After his treatment of you! Forget this foolish search, Ceres, and come home!"

"No."

"Ceres! There will be consequences. Come home now, and your punishment won't be as severe."

His voice, that tone, once sent shivers down my spine and twist my stomach in fear. Punishment? What more could he take? My dreams? My freedom?

"Try to stop me."

"Ceres!" I end the call.

With each careful step, I descend the rocky face of the cliff, reaching the bottom of a natural opening in the rock face. Concrete laid on the ground directs the stormwater into the river.

Standing at the mouth of the cave, I see the city's lights across the river, scaring all the stars away for the night. It's a mesmerising sight, hidden away along the rock of the Brisbane river.

Water streams down the cave, following the rocky bed formed by years of erosion, all leading out to the river. With each step deeper into the cave, my shoes become drenched in cold water. The light from the city vanishes, and pure darkness envelops me.

The rock walls, jagged as if naturally formed over years, are adorned with colourful spray-painted art, word art, and unintelligible squiggles. High-pitched squeaks of flying bats weave around me towards the exit, eels hiding in deep pools of water within the rock crevices.

As I venture further into the cave, the smell of bat guano assaults my nostrils, burning deep into my senses. Pushing through, dodging more flying creatures, I reach the start of the old red-brown brickwork laid over a century ago. I marvel at the entrance, contrasting starkly with the natural rock.

Before I step onto the brickwork, a giant lever protrudes from the rock wall. Spray-painted words read, *'Pull for magic.'*

Two halves of my mind wage war. Do I pull the lever or keep walking? What could go wrong? Would I miss my chance to find Zack? Surely someone would have mentioned this place if it were common knowledge.

With a shaky breath, I grasp the cold steel and pull.

The tunnel groans and creaks as gears come to life within. The entrance rumbles and stone bricks shift as an enormous staircase descends from above the pipe wall, hitting the ground with a light tap. Rhythmic beats of techno music emanate from within. This isn't the magic I was hoping for.

Gagging at the tainted air, I proceed, taking solid steps on the steel staircase. One after another, I reach the top and face four walls and a door.

A sudden creak and crunch lift the staircase, sealing the entrance. Steeling my nerves, I approach the door, grasp the cold knob, and swing it open.

My jaw drops as I'm met with bodies dancing, people drinking, music thumping, and the club bathed in a red tinge from the glow of luminescent lights. The sickly sweet smell of iron assaults my nose. I edge around the dancefloor, weaving and dodging past icy bodies. My skin crawls as I feel lingering eyes on me from the booths. I reach the bar.

My stomach twists as I see IV bags hanging in the bar fridge. Tearing my gaze from the unsettling sight, I'm met with something worse: a human treated like a juice box on a hot summer's day, their life fading as the creature holds them in an iron grip, guzzling every last drop.

An icy hand on my shoulder snaps my attention. Black painted nails rest on my skin, scars painting the pale flesh. Jagged and erratic. Hands, arms, legs, neck, shoulders, and one running from the eye to the lips.

Sharp fangs smile at me, red eyes filled with mirth, and dread consumes me.

"Now, how did you get in here?" I keep my mouth shut, scanning the club for an exit. "Don't bother," his smile fades.

"I'm looking for Zack." His eyes widen slightly in recognition. "Don't waste my time. Where is he?" His claws retract, and I notice my skin stitching itself together. He licks my blood from his claws, grimacing in disgust.

"What are you?"

"Last I checked, human, unfortunately."

A chuckle escapes his lips, and a bloody grin forms on his face. "Come with me."

He leads me further back, reaching for a single black door. If not for the guard, I might have mistaken it for the wall.

The rhythmic thumping outside is all I can hear in the backroom. It's spacious, with black padded lounge chairs on either wall, a mini bar at the back, and a desk sitting comfortably in the middle.

"Your friend came here five days ago," he sighs, sitting at the desk. "Humans can't get in without a supernatural with them." He leans back in the leather armchair, pulling out his phone. "You shouldn't be able to get in, but here you are." His fingers type rapidly, and he puts the phone to his ear. "Hey, we have a problem."

I watch the scarred man explain my appearance. He studies me as he listens carefully to the voice on the other side.

"Alright," he breathes and finally hangs up. "Do you understand what's happening?" I shake my head.

"I just came looking for my friend." He eyes me, clearly sceptical.

"If what you're saying is true, I find it hard to believe, considering you got in here." He shifts back in his seat. "Do you have an idea of what we are?"

"Considering the red eyes, fangs, and that scene earlier, I'm going to take a wild guess and say vampires." The corner of my lips quirk up.

"That we are. I own this club, and like I said, humans can't get in here without us. So my question is, what are you?" I shrug.

"If I knew, I would tell you. But this," I wave my hands around the room, "Is all new. Luca, my temporary therapist who's apparently a Magiq, practically ruined my whole sense of reality by revealing magic is real."

"Luca?" he raises an eyebrow.

"My 'Magiq therapist.'" I bend my fingers in quotation. Hoping not to sound crazy.

"Ah yes, the neutral term the current generation has made for their kind," he snorts, standing up and grabbing a drink from the mini-fridge. "We need to get to the surface. My brothers will be waiting for us." A sharp click and the grinding of gears moves the grey concrete wall aside. A steel ladder disappears into the roof above. "After you."

Chapter 14

Dread fills me as I reach the surface. I stand on solid pavement atop the mountain cliff of kangaroo point, waiting with the vampire. He looks over the Brisbane river, drink still in hand.

"It's always a pretty view from here," he remarks to no one. I maintain my distance, watching the road for any approaching cars.

A black car slows and pulls up to the curb. The driver's and passenger's doors open.

The driver leans against the car, arms crossed, and the passenger approaches me. His expression bored as if he's turning up for a math lesson. A sense of oppression envelops me, my senses screaming danger. I pause, focusing on steadying my rapid heartbeat and breathing slowly.

Straightening up, his pale lips form a friendly smile. The tense stare softens, and the strange sense of danger fades. "So, you're the girl he can't stop talking about," he reveals his sharp fangs.

"I might be." A steely glare replaces his sweet smile.

"Your friend has been moping since he woke up, and frankly, it's becoming annoying," he notes with a tired voice.

He inhales deeply and exhales sharply. The frosty glare dissipates, leaving a neutral expression. He mumbles something incoherent to himself, too fast or too low for me to catch.

"Where is Zack?" A burst of bravery surging within me. The vampire snaps out of his thoughts, his intense red eyes locking onto mine. Amusement glints in them, his lips curving into a small smile once more. The burst of bravery fades, allowing fear resurfacing.

"I intended to bring you to him, but…" He starts, and suddenly we are face to face. His cold eyes bore into me, sending shivers of fear deep into my soul with just a gaze. "What are you?" A hint of fang showing. I shudder under his scrutiny.

"I don't know. I'm trying to figure that out myself." I ignore the pit of dread in my stomach. The creature snarls.

"You smell different." He waves his hand in the air, searching for the right words. "It's unusual, and your heart beats slower than a human's." I release my held breath, shivering in the exhale.

"Her blood tastes strange too," the scarred vampire interjects.

"Really, Scar?" he scolds.

"What? It was just a taste." The creature in front of me relaxes, studying my expression before sighing.

"If you haven't realised, your friend has become a vampire, and he hasn't stopped talking about you either." He turns toward the car. "If you want to see your friend, I suggest you come with me," he walks towards the door.

"And if I refuse.".

"Then I'll have to kill you. It would be unfortunate for your friend, but given your anomaly, I won't hesitate." The vampire stands by the car. I watch the two vampires, my heart racing. "Scar." The vampire hums in acknowledgment. "Are you joining us or staying?"

"I'll stay. I have a club to manage." he smiles and walks to the cliff's edge, then jumps off. My jaw drops.

Do you want to see Zack? I take another breath and straighten my back, walking down the concrete path, ready to face whatever lies ahead. The other vampire opens the passenger door at the back for me. I get a closer look and notice his long brown hair tied up in a neat ponytail. He smiles at me and climbs into the car.

"I thought I was driving?" the vampire who threatened me inquires.

"It's my car, I'm driving," the long-haired vampire asserts as he gets in.

"I am an excellent driver," the other settles into the passenger's side. I ignore the bickering vampires and slide into the back seat.

"Oh, I know. I just prefer driving my car."

"Sook." I suppress my smile and hide my face from the vampire. I can't let him see my amusement.

"So, Ceres." the pony tailed vampire addresses me. My attention snaps up, and the vampire's eyes meet mine.

"How do you know my name?" the vampire chuckles.

"You're kidding, right? As soon as Zack woke up, it was 'Ceres this' and 'Ceres that.' He almost attacked me when he awoke."

"Not that he could have done much, given your strength," the other vampire interjects.

"And do you two have names? Or shall I refer to you as 'long-haired vampire' and 'vampire who threatened me,' or maybe 'vampire one and two'?"

"Who would be one? I assume I'm one since I'm driving," the first vampire argues.

"Don't be ridiculous, I'm one, you're two. I met her first," the other counters.

"But I was the one to open the car door for her, so that gives me the right," the long-haired vampire contends. As I listen to them bicker, their nature seems almost natural. They don't feel like blood-sucking monsters, but just regular people. "Besides, it's rude not to introduce ourselves, especially since you're willing to get into a car with us," the long-haired vampire shakes his head. "What did the government teach you? Didn't they tell you not to get into a stranger's car?" he sighs, and the other rolls his eyes.

"I don't know what you mean by the government, but yes, Nic did mention that."

"Yeah, him! He works for them. I thought they would have briefed you about us or something."

"They didn't... wait, Nic knows about vampires?" I lean forward, trying to grasp the situation. What am I hearing? Nic was aware of all this?

"Oh, well, yes. Nic knew all about us. He and that werewolf mutt, with their little team have been trying to eliminate us and our kind. Sorry you had to find out this way," he shrugs. "I thought since Nic looked after you, he would have told you."

"Obviously, that wasn't the case," the other vampire interjects.

"It's… ok… I guess." Unsure of what to say. "Besides, I only got into this car because I want to see Zack but don't think it was because you threatened me," I point at the vampire in the passenger seat.

"It's nothing personal, just a precaution," the vampire shrugs.

"He'll be glad to see you. He's been on my case about it," the long-haired vampire chimes in. "Oh, the name's Hawkeye," he adds with enthusiasm. "Sourpuss next to me is my older brother, Syrus."

"Gee… thanks," Syrus sighs and digs into his pockets, pulling out his phone.

"Hawkeye, like the show?" Hawkeye laughs.

"Nah, it's a great show, though. Surprised you know about it, but it's actually a nickname. I prefer not to have people know my real name."

"And you, Syrus, is that a nickname too?" Syrus remains silent and shrugs, still scrolling through his phone.

"Don't mind him. He's just annoyed we have a newborn in his home," Hawkeye teases, and Syrus retaliates with a punch to Hawkeye's shoulder.

During the trip, I stay silent, focusing on my breathing, counting every intake and outtake. In, out, in, out, one, two, three, four. My heart beats heavily and slowly, but adrenaline still courses through my veins, churning my stomach with each passing minute. Despite my attempts to distract myself by looking out the window, I can't calm myself down in a car with two vampires.

I watch the people moving through the streets, the twinkling lights, the life pulsing into the city as night falls. There's always something happening in the city.

I've always wanted to live in Brisbane, to escape the suburban life. The sense of community in small towns has always irked me. In the city, you're just another face, easily slipping through the cracks and becoming just another person in the crowd, perfect for anyone wanting to hide.

"Don't forget about the speed camera," Syrus mutters, still engrossed in his phone.

"I'm usually the one who has to remind you. I had to pay a hefty fine because of your driving."

"Is that why I, I'm not allowed to drive?" Syrus ignores Hawkeye's complaint.

"Yes, and because it's my car!" He slows down the car and enters the underground parking.

"I was willing to pay the fine." Syrus exits the car once it's parked. Hawkeye follows, closing the door behind him. I choose to stay inside, half-hoping they've forgotten about me.

"You coming?" Hawkeye asks, opening my door.

The stale air of the underground parking lot fills my lungs as I swallow the dry spit in my mouth. Nodding to Hawkeye, I step out and my foot meets the concrete floor, and a wave of dread washes over me. An icy shiver runs up my spine. The dim overhead lights cast long shadows, revealing rows of parked cars, their sleek surfaces reflecting the faint glow.

As we venture further into the lot, a wave of dread washes over me. The echoing sound of my footsteps reverberates off the bare walls. Yet, amidst the silence, I sense a presence lingering in the shadows. It's similar to Syrus' aura, but more sinister. Whispers seem to emanate from the concrete, growing louder with each step I take.

Cursing my existence, warning their sire of me. What is happening? Who are these beings on the walls, and why do they detest me so much?

Hawkeye leads the way to three different elevators, approaching the middle one, the metal doors gleaming under the harsh fluorescent lights. Inside the metal box, and with a swipe of his keycard, the last button on the top glows a dark red. He presses the button. Ninety-one floors to go.

The whispers accompany the soft hum of the elevator's ascent. They intensify with each level, their sweet threats growing more violent by the second.

"Shut up," I mutter under my breath. Syrus glances at me from the corner of his eye.

"You hear them?" he queries as the elevator doors open.

The apartment is massive, occupying the entire floor of the building. It's clear why the elevator serves as the main entrance. This place is designed to utilise every bit of available space.

To my right is an open-plan lounge, large enough to accommodate a massive lounge chair arranged in a 'U' shape, and a large flat-screen TV mounted on the wall beside me. I notice game controllers and mugs, possibly once filled with coffee or blood, left on the coffee table.

A young teen sits in the middle of the lounge, engrossed in his phone. He wears a hooded jacket, the lazily sits on his head, barley covering him and obscuring his blonde hair. A rose and two helix piercings adorn his right and left ears along with a dangling cross piercing. His red eyes briefly acknowledge us as we enter the apartment before returning to his phone.

"Hey, dad," he greets nonchalantly.

"Hey," Syrus responds, making his way to the kitchen. The lounge seamlessly transitions into the kitchen, neatly tucked under the staircase. Adjacent to the stairs is a doorway leading to a darkened hallway, which I avoid.

Past the kitchen is an elegant dining table, capable of seating twenty people. A balcony wraps around the building, with expansive glass windows showcasing the city skyline.

I'm slightly puzzled. Why would vampires need an oven and stove? A fridge makes sense, but the rest? "Has he been any trouble?" Syrus asks the teen. The young vampire shakes his head.

"No, just sulking upstairs, waiting for this human to appear." he points at me with his gloved hand.

"I wouldn't say she's exactly human," Syrus mutters, then sighs. "But I suspected as much. Coffee? Tea?" he offers to the room.

"I'll have some tea, if you have any," Hawkeye responds, swiftly collecting the empty mugs and playfully pulling back the teen's hood.

"Hey!" the teen protests. Hawkeye chuckles. The vampire readjusts his hood and looks at Syrus. "Any blood packs in the fridge?" he inquires.

"Just one. Rune, did you almost finish them all?" Syrus chides.

"Maybe." Rune gives a sly grin. "Couldn't be bothered hunting," he ducks behind the couch. Syrus groans and shuts the fridge.

"If you're going to be lazy, then you can go get more."

"Fine. But can I have a mocha, please?" Rune gives the biggest, sweetest smile he could muster, followed by feigned innocence. Syrus shakes his head before reluctantly agreeing. Turning to me, Syrus asks, "Ceres?"

"Coffee, please," I reply. Syrus nods and activates the coffee machine.

Suddenly, I hear a familiar voice. "Ceres!" In an instant, I'm enveloped in a hug. The scent of fallen rain is unmistakable. I feel the cold skin against mine, the lack of a heartbeat, the vice-like grip that doesn't hurt but is noticeably strong. I stand frozen, unsure whether to return the embrace. It feels odd to be hugged by another person… how long has it been since I last experienced this?

I look up into the face filled with happiness and tears. He wipes his eyes, which are no longer warm hazel but a terrifying, cold red with slit pupils. I should feel happy or empathetic that he's crying for me, but a surge of anger courses through me. I punch him in the face, and his head snaps to the side. He winces, cradling his jaw.

"Heh, nice," Rune chuckles, intently observing the unfolding scene.

"Hawkeye, Rune, can I see you both in the study?" Syrus calls out. Accepting the cue,

Hawkeye departs, making his way down the dark hallway. Rune momentarily protests.

"But, but," he halts as Syrus raises an eyebrow. Frustrated, Rune growls at the older vampire and storms off. Syrus gives both Zack and me a nod before leaving us alone.

"I probably deserved that," Zack admits, stroking his cheek. "You've always had a powerful punch, even now." Overwhelmed with emotions, I envelop him in a tight hug. Initially hesitant, Zack reciprocates, holding me close. Tears stream down my face, a mix of relief and pain flooding through me.

"You're safe."

"I'm safe." He tightens his embrace.

"You could have told me.".

"You'd have thought I was insane, claiming the need to become a vampire or that they exist. You'd have dismissed it," he murmurs into my hair. "But I felt so out of place…in my skin, as a human. As a vampire, I finally feel whole."

"This doesn't make any sense." my mind reeling as he holds me closer.

"I know. I wish I could've explained earlier, wish things were different." his grip firm yet comforting. "That man, Nic," Zack growls, a deep anger surfacing. "He obstructed every attempt to tell you the truth, threatening to turn your life into a nightmare."

"Nic?" My voice is a mere breath.

"Yes, Nic was the reason I had to keep my distance. I feared what he might do to you. The thought of causing you harm was unbearable."

"But you left without a word!" My voice breaks. "You left, and it hurt so much." Zack stays silent, simply holding me tighter.

"I'm so sorry," his voice quivering. "The fear of losing more people I care about to him…I couldn't risk you." His embrace tightens.

The intensity of the moment hangs heavy between us, a mix of sorrow, relief, and unresolved questions swirling in the air.

Then my phone rings. A loud buzzing, vibrating in my pocket. I groan removing myself form Zacks embrace and check to see Nics name on screen.

"He's not going to stop till I'm back," I hang up on his call.

"You can stay here. It's safe. They won't dare to touch this place!" I shake my head.

"No. I don't want to put you at risk. You've done enough to protect me. Now let me protect you."

"Ceres?"

"Right now, he thinks I'm still searching for you. We need to pretend as if I am still looking."

"His Organisation has eyes everywhere, they're going to know!"

"They won't." Syrus steps from the shadows of the wall, his arms crossed behind his back. "I'll make sure they'll never know," he gives a fanged smile. My heart leapt from my chest and an icy chill runs down my spine.

"H-how did you do that?" my voice breaks.

"I have my ways."

"You could just stay here," Zack repeats in a mumble. I grab his hand and give it a tight squeeze.

"I know, but right now, this is what I need to do. We'll come up with something." Zack looks to his feet before giving a small nod.

"All right."

Chapter 15

Year 2012

Zack fell to his knees, the old red brick building before him an inferno. The stench of burning flesh overwhelmed his senses. His chest ached with the loss of the vampires he'd come to know over the last three months. He'd thought he'd found his coven, his family, but now it lay in ashes.

"Third one this year?" The deep, familiar voice behind him broke the spell. Zack turned, eyes brimming with tears.

"Why?" Zack's hands clenched into fists.

"The answer is pretty obvious," Nic sneers, kicking Zack onto his back and pressing his heel into the teen's shoulder. "You're like a beacon. Vampires flock to you, making it so much easier to find them."

Zack struggled against Nic's weight. "Bastard."

"If I let you become one of them, I'd be failing my job," Nic shrugged, his heel

pressing down harder. "But I can overlook your existence and leave any group you find next alone." Zack froze, his own soul screaming to take the take the deal and finally be whole. "Leave Ceres. Distance yourself, and I'll overlook everything."

"Never! I'll never leave her!" Nic delivered a sharp kick to Zack's ribs.

"I suspected as much. Then consider option two." Nic leaned closer, his grip tightening in Zack's hair. "Stay away, or I'll make her life unbearable. The hardships she's facing now will pale in comparison to what I have planned if you don't leave." Nic laughed as watches the turmoil unfold within Zack. "It's always the same with you," Nic taunts. "Just one word of her you unfold. Too easy."

"If you touch her, I swear—" Zack winced as Nic's grip intensified.

"I won't, as long as you stay away," Nic growled, the threat clear. "You have one day to decide." Releasing Zack's hair, Nic walked away, leaving him in front of the burning remnants. Zack's thoughts spiralled out of

control. The thought of leaving his best friend rips a hole in his heart. Tears trickled down Zack's face as he watched the future he'd envisioned go up in smoke. The weight of an impossible choice thrusted upon him. The loss of his coven pains him, but the cost of his connection with Ceres terrified him.

Ceres, he thought. Forgive me.

Chapter 16

As I glance back, a sharp pain stabs my chest while the black car vanishes. Despite my longing to stay, I must confront Nic. Crossing the threshold, I tread down the familiar white hall, dread pooling in my stomach, a constant jittery buzz beneath my skin. I could never relax in this house.

In the lounge room, Nic waits, arms crossed, fury emanating from his eyes. "Where have you been?"

"Searching for Zack," my voice taut.

"And why didn't you return as instructed?"

"Because I didn't want to!" I take a defiant step forward. "I'll continue to search for him until I'm certain of his safety," I assert, the ache in my jaw sharpening. Nic steps back, a whiff of fear filling the air. "So, go ahead, make your worst punishment. I won't cease until he's safe." Nic swallows, a crack appearing in his façade as he crumbles under my gaze.

"Your internet access is restricted. You'll use it only for assessments, and I'm locking out all social media. You'll travel directly to school and back," his voice wavers. I smirk, undeterred.

"Fine. But my search for him continues." I storm upstairs to my room, no longer intimidated by his threats.

Post-school, I journey into the city and relay the sentence over in my head.

'Come over and we can go through your math.' He had to insist on it being math. Entering the apartment building, the atmosphere shifts. An eerie undertone of dark whispers float in the air and an icy chill wraps around my ankles like snakes. I look down to see nothing but my shadow stretched out on the polished stone. The closer I am to the light, the greater my shadow became.

The receptionists catch my eye as I make my way to the elevator. Their gazes are sharp, as if they're assessing more than just my presence. A reminder of the dual of the façade this place wields.

Owned by Syrus, this building is no ordinary residence but a sanctuary for those like him, veiled under the guise of an upscale apartment complex. The receptionists, more than mere administrative staff, serve as the first line of defence, while maintaining the secrecy of its unique inhabitants.

I swallow my unease and enter the steel box.

Reconnecting with Zack feels odd, as does visiting the vampires' abode. The dark whispers in the walls, foretelling my demise, they get louder and louder as I rise up in the complex, but they all seem to snuff out as I step over the threshold.

Standing in the afternoon light, Syrus greets me with a nod. "Afternoon Ceres."

My mouth drops as I see the vampire basking in the light, and begin wondering if the windows are UV resistant.

"Hi," I give a curt reply and look around for Zack. Syrus gives a small smile.

"He's hunting at the moment with Scar. He mentioned you would be coming. Please make yourself at home." He opens the sliding doors to let fresh air in. The rays did nothing to him. I see the content smile in the faint reflection of the glass.

"I'm guessing all those myths aren't true."

Syrus turns to me, his smile growing. "No. I suggest not to believe what you read or watch on television." He gives a nonchalant shrug. "But it is useful to keep the sheep misinformed." His smile darkens, exposing his fangs.

"Then what is real?" I sit on the lounge chair. "Religious artefacts?"

"No. If they did have an effect, then there would be gods, yes?" he shrugs.

"Running water?" Syrus laughs.

"No."

"Do you have the desire or urge counting rice or beans if they spill?"

"I hate that one, but no."

"Invitation to houses?"

"Breaking and entering is entertaining when hunting, gives them a false sense of hope," he grins.

"Garlic?"

"Tastes good on bread."

"Can you eat food?"

"We can, but it provides no nutrition."

"Animal blood?"

"Makes us sick over time. It tastes putrid." Syrus scrunches his nose up.

"Stake through the heart?"

"Hurts like a bitch, but no."

"Then how can you kill a vampire?" Syrus' smile falls, and he slowly approaches me.

"Why do you want to know?" a sharp glare cuts my way, and the surrounding air becomes oppressive. An icy chill crawls up my spine and felt something grip my throat.

"Considering my best friend is a vampire and is hunting people right now. You don't have to worry about me." The vampire continues to analyse me, looking for an inkling of a lie.

"And you're not bothered? Most humans would find an issue if they discovered their loved one became a blood-sucking vampire."

"No." This returns Syrus' smile. "I care about Zack and if he needs to eat people to live than I'm ok with it," I swallow my fear, finding my courage to speak my truth. "I don't care about humans, only the people who mean something to me." Syrus' eyes widen for a second before returning to their neutral gaze. The suffocating air leaves and the grip on my throat recedes. He approaches closer and places his hand on his chest.

"To kill a vampire, you either tear their heart out," he then grips his throat. "Cut off their heads or set us on fire."

"You guys are pretty tough to kill."

"We are, but it's not impossible. Just harder." Syrus concludes and the elevator doors signal their arrival. Zack walks out with a dopey smile on his face.

"Good hunt?"

"Yeah," he shuffles over to me and leans his head on my shoulder. "I missed you," he closes his eyes.

"I missed you too," A small smile graces my lips.

"Where's Scar? I thought he was coming back with you?" Syrus asks.

"He said he was going to check out this bar that just opened up for the vamp community." As he finished those words, Rune comes racing down the stairs towards the elevator.

"Bye Dad!" he shouts.

"Where are you going?" Syrus calls out.

"Out with uncle Scar to check out this bar."

"All right. Be safe, don't do anything stupid."

"I won't! I'm fifteen hundred years old. I know how to look after myself," he complains with a smile and steps in the elevator.

"I know." Syrus whispers with a pained voice. Watching the doors close and his son waves goodbye. "Now I believe you have studying to do. I'll be in my office."

It's just me and Zack now. His presence has made life more bearable. I even feel more at peace in Syrus's home, less hostile and irritable.

"Nic still believes you're looking for me?"

"Yep. I've defied his attempts to stop me. The guy struggles to get in my way," I snort. Zack chuckles, the image amusing him.

"Did you bring them?" he settles down onto the floor, legs tucking under the coffee table.

"Yes," I groan, pulling out textbooks from my bag. Zack's logical argument that graduation is my ticket out annoys me, but I comply. Facing my greatest adversary, math, sometimes feels more daunting than any other challenge.

I slump over the coffee table, my math book open before me, filled with amateur art and ancient scribbles. Occasionally, my gaze drifts to Zack, equally perplexed by his phone.

The apartment has become a sanctuary, away from school and the people I despise. I'm safe here, with the only person who matters.

"I hate math." Zack offers a smirk and a comforting pat on the back.

"You've got this." I stick my tongue out in response before reluctantly returning to the dreadful textbook. Eventually, I give up and look back at Zack with a plea.

"How about we swap? You take my math test, and I pass." Zack laughs, dismissing the idea with a shake of his head.

"I doubt I'd look good in a skirt. Plus, people think I'm dead, remember?" His words trigger a hearty laugh from me.

"Fair point," my smile fading as thoughts of the future creep in. The uncertainty of what lies ahead for us weighs heavily.

"You okay?" Zack notes my sudden shift in mood.

"What's going to happen to us?" The present seems too fleeting. I fiddle with my pencil, avoiding his gaze.

"I'm not sure," Zack closes his book and leans back. "These secret meet ups have been fun," a mischievous smile plays on his lips. "Got any plans for Friday night?"

"This Friday?"

"Yeah. I've got something in mind after your kendo test," his enthusiasm evident.

I tell him the test ends at eight, and he nods, the cogs in his head clearly turning with some plan.

"What?" I press, sensing he's up to something.

"Nothing," he replies too quickly. His smile returns. "Just thinking."

Chapter 17

Kendo ends, and the girls all clamour out of the studio, avoiding my gaze. Taking my time, I make my way to the exit. Some wait for their parents, others for ride-sharing, and some depart for the bus. I passed with flying colours. I worked so hard to get to this point; it would have been ridiculous if I didn't pass my ultimate test.

I recognise the familiar scent of rain and overhear some girls whispering about the cute boy outside the gate. I slow my pace to a stop and look up from my phone.

The grey beanie atop his crown, the red jacket, and the white shirt adorned with dream catchers. The grey scarf he wears for winters is wrapped around his neck. No longer does the weather affect him, and he can wear anything with comfort. His red eyes widen, darting down and then up. A noise escapes his lips, his voice getting caught in his throat. Zack panics and looks away. He coughs, clears his throat, and looks back at me. "You look… amazing."

I feel my cheeks heat, my face burning. It's been a long time since I felt warmth from my circulation.

"I'm just in my normal clothes." It's nothing special, just a singlet and skinnies. Though it is humid, I can easily wear jeans in the hot weather.

"You still look amazing," Zack grins. All the surrounding girls watch Zack and me interact, whispering among themselves, asking how I know the cute boy before me. "Ready for a fun night? I have so much planned!" I can't stop the smile forming on my face. My cheeks begin to burn, feeling like someone turned the summer heat on full blast within the muscles on either side of my face. My lips twitch as if they're about to give way. It feels like my face is about to crack. It has been a long time since I genuinely smiled. Pro: have a great time, be closer to Zack once more, enjoy a good time. Con: Him going on a rampage and eating people.

"What about your bloodlust?" I ensure no one around us hears. Zack gives a fanged smile.

"Don't you worry, I got that covered," he points behind him. I look to see no one there. I'm not convinced.

"Alright, is there anything I need to do?"

"Nope, just be you." I take a deep breath, smiling through the ridiculousness that is Zack Castellan, and enjoy the outing.

"So, what have you planned?"

"Well, I thought we'd get dinner first and then head into the city." I look at him with a raised eyebrow.

"And how are you…" I trail off as Zack maintains his smile.

"I have it all planned," he grins triumphantly. I sigh and shake my head at the young vampire.

"Okay, lead the way,"

Zack dramatically bows. "After you, m'lady." I roll my eyes, walking past him and through the gates.

"You're such a dork," I call out, and Zack laughs into the city night. Zack is a few steps ahead, turning back to me and walking backward. He gives me a big grin and slows down, waiting for me to catch up.

Side by side, we walk in silence, watching the cars drive by and letting the city's noise fill the empty space.

Zack stops without warning, looking both ways before crossing the street. I follow closely behind. Without uttering a single word, Zack leads me down a narrow alley.

"Ready?"

I look around and see nothing. The alley is cramped, with nothing here but two brick walls and graffiti art displaying Brisbane's many street artists. Zack clears his throat, his hand knocking on the painted blooming rose wall. The sound reverberates, sounding like wood.

A little slot opens up, revealing two bright yellow eyes gazing at us. "Ah, a table reserved under Scar." Zack's voice quivers with a nervous smile. The eyes widen and then close the slot, only to open the door. "After you." Walking in, my attention quickly diverts to the glass roof and the millions of stars shining in the dark sky. "Magiqs have a knack for manipulating random spaces in the world," Zack shrugs.

I look at the interior around me and see dwarf trees growing from the ground. Small paper lanterns hang on the branches, illuminating the field below, plants growing from the brick walls. The hardwood floor and dark brick complement each other, giving off a romantic setting for anyone who enters.

"How?"

"The magiq who owns it specialises in nature, finding it easy to grow plants in an indoor space."

"And the stars?"

"Magic."

"How? How do you know this place exists?"

"Word of mouth… well, more Scar telling me the places in the city," Zack coyly admits. "You like it here?" his voice softens, gently grasping my hand. I ease into the touch and nod.

"It's beautiful," Zack beams.

"I'm glad. I've wanted to show you this place for weeks." He looks away from me, refusing our eyes to meet. If he could blush, Zack would be pink.

A vampire approaches us, two menus in hand, greeting us both and leading us to a table. I see both vampires, humans, and magiqs all in the same room. Some humans dine with vampires, some eat alone, and others gather in tight-knit circles, deliberately keeping their distance from the vampires. Whispering slanders about them, but the vampires do not react.

We sit near the back, with a small table and two chairs on either side. Close to other vampires, fair enough from those with a heartbeat. The waiter gives us both menus, along with a glass filled with complimentary water and a small shot of blood. Zack thanked the waiter. They nodded without saying much and left us to decide what we wanted.

I see a human option and a vampire option over the menu. I can't help but read what they offer. Bagged blood is a complimentary drink and entrée mixed with alcohol. The main menu items are titled 'From vein to glass.' Live donors donate their blood to various soups containing blood sausage and other blood-related foods. Their desserts are blood made into cream and icicles. One dessert is just straight blood over ice. They consider it the most popular one. Talk about extortion.

"I never expected to see a restaurant catering to both diets."

"It's great, hey. Both species can enjoy a delightful meal together."

"Yet they could easily reach over and eat their date." Zack chuckles and nods.

"True, but when you like someone… you don't really want to eat them," his voice lowers to a whisper, his eyes looking away from mine once more.

"Fair, but you can just hunt for food without paying. I'm surprised you have to pay for this." I glare at the prices of the vampire menu.

"Not all humans are willing to donate for free. We all know that some want the peaceful route. Keeping away from hunters and not drawing trouble. We have the urge to satisfy a primal desire to kill, which is easily remedied after a hunt. Besides, it's easier when you want to take someone out on a date. It would be kinda awkward for you and me," he laughs nervously.

"This is a date?" I point out the one word that caught my interest, raising an eyebrow at him. Zack freezes, playing with his hands. Incoherent babbling escapes his mouth, and he looks anywhere but at me. I grab his hand and hold it. Zack looks up in surprise. He looks at me with wide eyes, the sudden contact startling him. I give him a warm smile, which seems to put him at ease.

"It's… nice… y'know. Coming here, with you, talking to you once more. It feels like old times." His long black bangs covering his cheeks, hiding his eyes.

"It does, doesn't it?" I feel the corners of my lips twitch up, cracking the stoic façade, appearing happy, but for the first time, I genuinely feel happy.

We're left in comfortable silence, eating our meals and watching people at their own tables, everyone laughing and smiling with their friends and loved ones. Music plays quietly in the background, carrying a calming peace to this moment, a calm I hadn't felt in a long time.

Chapter 18

"You got a C in math," Nic begins, eyes fixated on the chopping board in front of him. "Your grades haven't slipped since searching for that boy," he grits and slams the knife's edge down on the capsicum. "Though I would have preferred an A."

"You know, maths isn't my strong suit," I mutter, peeling the potato in my hands.

"I know. Hence why I'm surprised, and I thought they would go by the wayside." he waves his hands dramatically. Silence falls on us once again. I go over the passing week in my head, reflecting on the date, the class', the existence of vampires. It's all a whirlwind and I've just been staying afloat. Hadn't had time to think or process. What would Luca say if they were here? Would they laugh and say this is normal? It doesn't matter really, magic exists and so does the supernatural, so do I want to be in a boring organisation? Living a nine to five? No. I don't even want to be tied down, having to think about another person's opinion other than my own. I want to be the one to call the shots.

"Ceres," Nic breaks through my thoughts. "Let's just forget this hostility. I miss being able to talk to you and hear about your days." I still and bite my tongue. "I want us to be on good terms, as before Zack's disappearance." I don't know what to say or even how to react to this plea. Nic continues to prep for dinner but sighs out loud. "Have you given any thought to working for Hidebound Corp?" he asks. "I don't want it to be awkward when you start working there and we're fighting." He gives a light chuckle. "It will be great; we can carpool together… though I already drive you everywhere," Nic rambles on. "You will get great experience. There are opportunities to move up in the corporation, and you can make new friends …. Maybe meet a nice guy… or girl."

"I told you I'm not into girls."

"Ah! Right, I forgot, you said you're… a… ace…," stumbling over his words, trying to remember what I tell him.

"Grey Asexual."

"Right! And you're only into guys," he nods, agreeing with his thoughts. "I don't get how this all works, but hey, whatever floats your boat." His joke makes me roll my eyes. Heaving another sigh and looking back at the man. Still rolling the dough, flattening it into a nice thin base. Directing my attention to the sink, I pick up another potato. I feel my heart sink, aching in my chest, making it hard to breathe.

"I've been thinking." Nic hums in response. "I don't want to work for Hidebound." Silence falls between us once more.

"What made you come to this conclusion?" his voice levelled like steel.

"I want to find my path… as grateful as I am for the opportunity… I just feel like I need to do things my way," I put the peeled potato down on the board. Nic sighs loudly and slams the cupboard door shut. I jump out of my skin and turn to the furious human.

"Eight years. I've been working on you for eight years, and this is the result I get…" he exhales loudly. "I should have listened, but no, I was stubborn to think I could change your thinking," Nic looks at me, his eyes burning with rage. I lean back on the counter, feeling the knife behind me. "I tried, I really did. I could have saved eight years of my life and went with their original plan," Nic grumbles, his hand covering his face. A shot of guilt hit me in the chest. "I guess we'll have to do it their way," he busts out a giggle, smiling to himself. I feel fear rise in my chest, my hand gripping the knife, ready to defend myself. Nic takes another step closer. A growl rises from my chest, a dull ache pulses through the top of my jaw. "Just like them, when cornered, you will always bare your teeth." his hand digging into his pocket.

"Sorry, Nic," I grip onto the knife. My focus narrows and I charge. The knifes blade gleams and the sharp edge aiming for his shoulder. All with the purpose of doing harm, then kill. Nic bears through the pain with a grimace, his eyes locking onto mine.

"Should have aimed for the throat," he breathes. Words laced with pain. A sharp, icy sting stabs into my shoulder. A serum potent and reactive burins into my system. My pulse quickens, fear and poison pumping through my veins. The world around me blurs into a haze, and my legs buckle beneath me, causing me to collapse. Gasping for air, I can feel the strain in my chest, as if my lungs are desperately trying to expand. "Snake venom," Nic pulls the knife out of his shoulder. "It won't kill you. Just keep you weak."

"Fuck... you," I manage to snarl. The beast breaks from its cage, my teeth sharp and lengthen, baring them to the human before me.

"There it is," he waves his hands in the air. "The beast, you've been fighting for so long, disappointing," Nic kicks me in the ribs. I fall to the ground. Limbs turning to jelly. "I really did like you, Ceres, truly. I was really hoping you would say yes, make it easier for both you and me."

I rise from the floor, bringing forth strength from within. "If you really cared, you would hope for me to be happy," I breath through the pain.

I am only met with a blank face. Uninterested and uncaring about my plea.

"What you wanted never mattered," Nic grabs his phone from his pocket, quickly texting a message and putting it away. "The training, the lessons, the therapy, the long nights dealing with your nightmares, the accident," my blood runs cold, and fury ignites in my chest. I ignore the burning sensation, pushing through the pain, and I strike. My hand transforms into dangerous claws, reaching for his throat.

Both bodies collapse to the floor. Nic stills under me as I grip onto his throat. Warm blood flushes between my fingers.

"You fucking bastard!" I cry out, my voice breaking with loss. I raise my fist and taking a swing at Nic's face. He snaps his head to the side, his skull cracking and blood pouring from his mouth. "You killed them!" I whimper, my hands shaking. "I had a home, a family and you took it all away from me!" I scream. "You took my home, my freedom, everything!" Nic remains frozen, unbothered. "Just once, I wanted you to ask what I wanted. Ask if I wanted to see someone or go through training, anything, but you didn't. You just signed me up, telling me how good it would be for me. Not once did you care to ask." Tears flow down my cheeks. The droplets fell off my face and onto Nic's shirt. Nic blankly stares at me through his lidded eyes, his lips set into a thin, straight line.

"Sorry," he says without an inkling of remorse. "But my cause is more important than your happiness." My eyes widen, and my chest twists painfully, crushing under the weight of my emotions. Nic's arm swiftly moves and jabs another needle full of venom. Plunging into my system once more, my body feels like it's set alight. Poison coursing through my veins like liquid fire.

Nic pushes me off as if I was a paper bag in the breeze. I roll onto my back and watch him loom over me.

"Why?" Feeling the second dose of venom course through me. "Why did you go to all this effort?" I grit, trying to find my footing, and stumble over again. My stomach churns, and chills go down my back.

"You really haven't figured it out?" his voice laced with disbelief. "The prejudice towards humans, your sharp claws, incredible healing, acute hearing, and strength to overpower a grown man." He shakes his head in dismay. "You're the world's only hybrid, the perfect fusion of human and vampire. That's why we want you. We've gone through so much trouble to get to you, to use you as the ultimate weapon to destroy those parasites." Words escape my throat as my brain flatline, losing all ability to think. "Using you is our path to eradicating them," Nic concludes.

"Killing my parents doesn't make it right," I snarl, baring my now-sharpened teeth.

"Two innocent people are dead because of you!"

"Even our organisation must sacrifice a few to save many. Do you understand the havoc those creatures wreak?" Nic snaps. "Families destroyed, bodies mangled and mutated for their simple pleasures. We're mere food to them, and I've witnessed my fair share of death at their hands. I'm willing to do whatever it takes to destroy them."

"So your plan is to trap me here and force me into your bidding?" I stand, a testament to my will. Nicolai glares at me.

"I'll admit, your resilience has always impressed me. No matter the situation, you always find a way to keep fighting." He smirks. "But I had hoped you'd be the perfect soldier, willing to be part of our cause. A weapon that doesn't question our motives." His voice turns bitter as he punches me in the face. "Instead, I got a defiant, arrogant teen who fights me at every turn, unwilling to appreciate the path I laid out for you."

"You believe you did what's best for me?" I roar. "You ripped my family away, isolated me, stripped me of joy because it was a 'distraction,' lied to me and forced me into these programs under the guise of 'what's good for me.'" I rise again, evading his attack and strike, grabbing hold of his waist and my claws digging into Nic's lower spine. Piercing the nerves and embedding deep into his tissue. Nic yowls in agony, his legs spasm and collapse under him. He hits the floor but remains determined, crawling. I take a moment to catch my breath, stepping back. "You're really not going to give up, are you?" Nic drags himself across the floor, his legs now dead weight.

"Wherever you go, I'll follow." He vows. "The people you care about will die because of you and what you are," he grinds out between clenched teeth.

"Does that make you any better than them?" Nic remains silent, continuing his desperate crawl. "You'd kill everyone just to control me. That's why your organisation disgusts me. I value freedom, Nic, you know that," he ignores me and grabs at my ankle. With a sigh, I wrench it free and stomp on his hand. He screams, bones snapping under my shoe. "To repay you for wasting your human years on me, I'll let you live." Nic laughs, a dark, mad glint in his eyes.

"You pity me, creature," he spits.

"Consider it, as a thanks for raising me," my voice cold as ice.

My body weakens, shutting down slowly. The venom courses through my veins, my nerves screaming in pain, my lungs burning with each gasping breath, and my vision darkening. As I collapse to the floor, the last thing I see are armed guards bursting into the kitchen.

Fuck.

Chapter 19

The sudden sound of boots against the concrete floor yanks me from my slumber. Each thunderous stomp echoes in my ears, with rubber screeching against the concrete. The chill seeps through the thin fabric of my clothes. My fingers stiffen and my body aches.

"Keep my distance?" I overhear the guard mumbles, his voice lace with scorn. "You're joking, right? What's some little girl gonna do?" he grunts, his heavy boots stomping closer to the bars. A loud clang hits the metal and echoes through. No one replies to the guard's scorn. "Fucking pathetic. How is this little shit meant to fight vampires?" The familiar bubbling of rage rips through my chest, ready to bare its fangs and draw blood.

Before the guard can utter another word, I grip the man's throat, my claws digging into flesh, and the sickly scent of iron coating the musty underground air. His eyes widen, and he aims the gun at me. I rip it from his hands and crush the barrel. "Give me the keys and I won't end your pathetic life," I hiss, tightening my hold. The guard struggles against my grip, moving and twisting his body like a snake caught in a trap. A low growl escapes my lips, and my claws tear deeper into his flesh. Blood flows from his throat like a waterfall, and the room begins to spin. My stomach churns, and I feel the burning acid rising to my throat.

With a swift tug, I tear the flesh from the guard's throat, holding the bloody mass in my hands, watching him fall to the ground and bleed out. The guard emits a wheeze, blood bubbling from his throat as the air escapes his lungs.

A cruel grin spreads across my lips as I watch the last glimpses of his life leave his eyes. The thrill of the kill runs down my spine, urging me to find more. Tear them limb from limb, let their blood paint the white walls, hear their screams for mercy as I cut them down one by one.

I drop the flesh and stare at the red coat of blood on my hand. I tremble, darting back to the dead body outside the cell, my hand, the blood. Static overwhelms my brain, and the bile escapes my lips.

"Fuck," I curse, spitting out the remnants of my lunch. "I didn't mean to, I didn't," I whisper over and over. "Fuck, fuck, fuck!" I shout.

With shaken hands, I reach through the bars and fish for the keys.

I wince as the barred door lets out a loud moan. I step over the body, afraid if I look back, I wouldn't have the strength to leave.

Like a mouse trapped in a maze, I navigate the underground halls of the facility. They all blur together, corridors and corridors of monochrome white shape and become as one. Each turn I took is the same two walls laughing at me. Whether they had padded cells or an abode of doors, I felt like I was going in circles. The halls all look the same. I halt, catching the silvery difference in the walls. My heart jumps to my throat, as chance, a way out.

I skid to a halt, catching my breath. I hear it echo for miles in the long halls. Look to my left, a glimmer catches my eye. A subtle deviation from the white walls in the depths at the end. A faint silvery sheen.

Leaping like my heart, I push on. The surrounding walls change and become a metallic silver, all leading me to the last stretch of my escape. Freedom. I can finally see it. I half expect this to be a trap, but I ignore my fears and turn the last corner and see hope.

An elevator sitting proudly at the end of the sterile steel walls, its light blinking up and the buttons begging to be pressed. Without hesitation, I press the button profusely and anxiously wait for the elevator to arrive.

The loud ding signals its arrival and I jump in and slam the button for the doors and press for the ground floor. Hoping I made the right choice.

I burst throughout into the grand entrance like a horse on the racetrack and I am met with the chaos of battle. Guns firing, guards shouting and all run to surround me.

One figure stands out starkly against the backdrop of violence, Zack. His black hair, now matted with the crimson of human blood, serves as a chilling crown. His razor-sharp teeth, exposed and, sink mercilessly into the flesh of the enemy. His claws, lethal and precise, slice through the resistance offered by their padded armour as if it were mere paper.

He carves a path through the armed guards swarming around him. Bullets seem to either hit him and others some ricocheted off the metal lockdown doors.

A group of guards manage to overwhelm him, tackling him to the floor. Snapping me from my daze, a surge of adrenaline kicks in. I ignore the danger and race to save my friend. Pushing through the circle of guards.

"Stop her!" voices shout behind me.

With the years of rigorous training, I have honed my skills to instinctual precision. Each move, each decision in combat, came naturally to me as breathing. But nothing prepared me for the searing pain of bullets tearing through my flesh. Shock holts me. Looking to my side, I see the hole through my shirt, blood seeping through my wound, but something odder came about. The bullet pushes out of my body and the wound seal in seconds. Well shit.

A guard charges at me with a knife. channelling my shock and adrenaline, I dodge his swing. A swift kick send the guard flying and sprawling to the ground, his weapon clattering out of his reach.

I wrench the gun out of the hands of another and my hands sharpen into dangerous claws, slicing effortlessly through the padded armour, aiming for the throat, tearing the guard's paper skin apart.

This feeling, this resilience, my body changing and reacting in ways I never thought would happen. Injuries felt like nothing. The guards felt like toy dolls I could throw away easily. This fuels me to keep going.

Zack lets out a cry, his fangs bared, eyes crazed like a wild animal as they pin him to the floor. His vigour draining away as they surround him.

I freeze, panic gripping my throat as I watch him be injected with the same serum I was given. Without thought, my feet move, hands tearing flesh apart. The world became a blur, and all I could think of was to save my friend.

I feel the familiar sharp sting on the back of my shoulder. Veins set alight as the venom courses through me once more.

I fall to my knees, crawling to my friend, his eyes glassing over and body going slack. Guards swarming around me once again, and the last thing I see is the painted Hidebound Corporation Logo on the wall.

Chapter 20

I awake to a pair of white shoes lying next to me. The familiar burn coursing through my veins, reminding me of the agony I feel. I wanted it to stop. My lungs burn with every breath I take. I can feel the cold sheen of sweat all over my body.

"What are you doing here?" I ask his feet. A pained cough echoes within the cell.

"I came to rescue you," Zack winces, and I give a weak smirk.

"It didn't go according to plan." A light chuckle escapes my lips.

"No," Zack replies. "It didn't."

"What were you hoping?" Cutting him off. "Break in, fists swinging, bust me out and escape?"

"That's what I had in my head. Syrus found out where you were. I… I couldn't wait for a plan. I had to come."

"Did he know about this place before my capture?"

"He did." Zack heaves a cough before speaking again. "But he didn't want to risk an all out assault on them if it meant his own family was in danger. He wanted to wait."

"Answers my question about why he never did anything in the first place."

"What about you?" Zack coughs up another lung. "Bust out and just waltz through the front door."

"Yeah." I grin at the roof. "I got out of the cell, just wasn't expecting to get in again so soon."

"Looks like we both didn't think things through."

"Nope."

"I barely stood a chance," he sounds defeated. "Only got past the big doors, and humans overran me. I couldn't even get to you."

"We both aren't strong enough," I grimace. "How can either of us save the other if we cannot protect ourselves?" The truth hung in the air like led. It's not strength and fighting against hordes of guards, but the truth in our relationship.

How can we protect each other if we cannot protect ourselves? I can't keep relying on him emotionally and physically. Just as he can't with me. We both need to get stronger and to do that, we may need to be apart.

"We both need to get good." Zack moves his feet away from my head, a small moan soon after. "The smell of blood is driving me nuts." a rumble rose from his throat.

"Yeah. Sorry about that."

"It's not your fault. You don't smell appetising."

"Oh." My heart sinks. "So it's not because of the guard I killed." I swallow down the guilt, reminding myself they are the bad guys. Silence befalls us, and my heart begins to beat erratically.

"You ok?"

"I killed someone. I took his life," I whisper. "I became something else. There was no hesitation, only the instinct to be cruel, to take lives without a second thought."

"Hey, hey, hey," he cuts me off. "Don't forget what those bastards did to you. They took away your family, your life, and they were about to take your freedom!" he shouts.

His words can't quell the storm raging within me. I've crossed the line. The cold clarity of my actions, the ease with which I embraced that darkness, terrifies me more.

"I'm terrified of myself. Of the beast inside that didn't flinch at the cruelty, that revelled in the bloodshed." My voice cracks. "I'm becoming a monster."

"Your not a monster. You were defending yourself." Zack's voice falls to a whisper.

"Will it get easier?"

"The guilt? Maybe. Killing? It gets easier."

"Was it hard for you?"

"No," Zack answers without hesitation. "As soon as I awoke, I wanted nothing but blood and when I tasted it. Nothing mattered, not even the life attached to it. I just wanted the hunger sated, and when there was nothing left.

I felt pleasure, to take a life, to drink every drop of their blood. It's intoxicating."

"I felt so sick." My stomach churns and swallow the lump in my throat. "But a piece of me enjoyed it. Revelled in it."

"You're not exactly human, remember?" Zack reminds me. I nod.

"Doesn't make me feel any better."

"I know," he acknowledges. "But it's a reminder for you not to be too harsh on yourself. What you did was instinct."

"If you say so." I swallow the guilt and stare at the roof, noting all the small cracks in the concrete.

A hybrid. Me. That's what I am, after all this time. My sense of smell, unbridled strength, my agility, my ability to heal and not get sick and this desire … the caged beast beneath my breast, it had been waiting for so long and when I let it loose. Someone died. Am I ok with it? Am I okay with taking the lives of others into my own hands? Humanity has pissed me off so much, but to take action, I can't help but feel sick within myself.

How? How is all of this even possible? My parents are human. Were they even my parents? Did they lie to me this entire time? I need answers. Why don't I need blood to survive? Do I continue aging or will I stop? Can I live forever like them, or will my life be prolonged? None of this makes any sense. I am a freak.

All this time Nic just wanted the power I had, and become a tool in the end. A weapon with no choices, no thoughts, no feelings. Nothing. Just take orders and hope I die to gain true freedom. The fucking bastard never cared.

"Any plans on getting out of here?" Zack breaks my thoughts. I swallow the lump down my throat, blinking away the tears and breathe.

"No. you?"

"Well, if we're lucky, Syrus and the others will come to the rescue," Zack answers.

"And if they don't?"

"They will. I'm part of the coven now. They wouldn't leave me behind."

"How can you be certain? How did you even come across them in the first place?"

I hear Zack cough some more before answering. "Scar turned me. That immediately makes me part of the coven. As for how I met them, I wish it had been under better circumstances."

Chapter 21

Zack sits at the burnt building for hours. His shot at becoming complete is gone once more. He mourns the friends he made, all gone, turned to ash. Tears stream down his face like a never-ending waterfall, the hollowed ache in his chest becoming too much to bear. He would tear out his own heart, just to feel nothing. An icy chill runs down his spine, goosebumps prickling his skin as he senses a powerful presence.

"So, little Abeyant. Care to explain what happened?" a deep voice inquires.

"I-I didn't mean for it to happen. I-I never wanted this," Zack sobs. The vampire circles the young Abeyant, arms crossed behind his back. "I lost them," he whimpers. "I lost them all."

"Do you know who did it?"

"Them," Zack snarls. "That bastard Nic!" he punches his fist into the concrete, unconcerned with the pain shooting up his arm.

"Nic?" the vampire raises his brow, turning his head to the building, watching the dying embers fade away. "I take it Hidebound has been using you as a beacon?" Zack nods his head shamefully. "This explains the increased coven deaths."

Zack nods his head. The tears haven't stopped. Memories of the ones he called friends mock him behind his eyes. His chest weighs heavily as he looks back to the burning building. So many gone in the last year. Another chance to be whole, gone once more. "He said he would stop if I stayed away," Zack whispers.

"From whom?"

"My friend." Zack hears the vampire sigh.

A grim line sets upon the elder vampires lips, a storm brewing behind his ancient eyes. "We had a suspicion it was Hidebound and not a group of hunters." Syrus looks down at the broken Abeyant. "In the previous attacks, I thought everything was lost to the flames. Until the pattern presented itself." Syrus turns back and nods to his brother, Scar. "They're clever to use you and if we acted too quickly they may have killed you instead." Zack punches the concrete anger rising to the surface.

"Fucking bastard!"

"I understand your anger but with you here, we can take action. Scar." The vampire covered in scars emerges from the shadows. His expression shares the same sorrowful gaze towards the ashen building. "Can you take him home?"

Scar looks at the broken Abeyant. He doesn't move, only stares at Zack, his lips thinning, his eyes shifting between Zack, Syrus, and the burning building. Nodding to himself, he finally speaks. "I'll oversee his turning."

"Are you sure?" his older brother raises a brow. Scar nods.

"I am."

Chapter 22

I awaken to the sounds of screams echoing and gunfire in the dimly lit hall. My body feels like lead; every movement feels as if tiny people are trying to hold me down with ropes. A low, guttural snarl emanates from Zack's lips, his teeth bared to the air.

"Here's hoping it's the rescue team," I remark, coughing afterward.

We both hear the rustling of keys, metal clanging against metal amidst the gears and springs.

"Transfer them to a secure facility!" a guard shouts. Several footsteps race into the cell. Rough hands seize my shoulders, hooking under my arms and lifting me from the ground. A low rumble escapes my throat. The edges of my vision blur, blinking against the bright light burning into my cornea.

"Get your fucking hands off me," Zack's slurred words follow, accompanied by loud banging.

"Steady him!" they shout.

More screams echo down the hall, gunfire resonating in repetition. The guards hasten their steps, my body jostling in the air.

"Damn it!" they exclaim. I hit the ground with a heavy thud, my back aching. I wince and roll onto my side as they fire their guns. The screams of the fallen replace the fire of bullets, the smell of iron filling the air. Another low rumble comes from Zack, clawed hands scraping against the concrete as he pulls himself closer to a lifeless body. Drinking his fill.

A dark figure approaches, shrouded in shadow. Emerging from the darkness, red eyes gaze intently at me.

"I see we arrived just in time," a familiar monotone voice resonates before I lose consciousness once again.

Muffled voices and sounds enter my ears as my fingers regain feeling. Flexing them, I brush against the soft fabric. My body lies comfortably against a soft mattress, my head on a firm pillow. I take a deep breath, shifting my head and cracking my eyes open. The room is dimly lit, a blurred figure sitting still on a chair next to my bed. I blink a few more times, and the figure becomes clear as day. Zack, slumped in the chair, appears still as a statue, asleep. Though it doesn't look like he is. His chest is still; it's unnerving. He's undead; he doesn't need to breathe.

Slowly, I lift myself from the bed. My neck is stiff. I flex and twist to loosen the muscles. No longer aching, the venom no longer courses through my body. It's odd; I'm alive. I should be dead.

I remove the covers, sliding my feet over to the floor. Leaning forward, I gently place my hand on Zack's shoulder. "Hey."

Zack stirs at my voice. He groans and stretches in his seat, two pale grey eyes staring back at me, his pupils round and no longer terrifyingly slit.

"Hey," he croaks, lips forming a sleepy smile. I remain silent, my hand cradling his head, my thumb gently brushing over his cheek.

"Your eyes, they're not red," I observe. Zack leans into my touch, enjoying the warmth from my body.

"Mmm, hungry," is all Zack can manage before closing his eyes again. "Couldn't eat, not knowing if you'd be okay." I offer a weak smile. Idiot.

"How long was I unconscious?"

"A day." Zack can barely open his eyes again.

"You get that hungry?"

"Newborn, remember. I'll be like this for three months, six at most," he gives a sleepy smile.

"Kind of sucks, not gonna lie." Zack shrugs and leans his head on the mattress.

"It is what it is."

"Come on, let's get you some blood." I rise from the bed. Zack follows with drawn-out steps, his eyes threatening to shut again as we reach the door.

I'm met with a long, lit hallway, stairs at the very end, and on either side of the hallway are two doors juxtaposed from each other.

Before I take a step onto the dark varnished wood, Rune emerges from the door to my left. Dressed in black pyjamas, his blonde hair messily sprawled, eyes barely open. He looks at me with a grimace.

"I should have stayed in bed," he mumbles, trudging towards the staircase. With a sigh, I follow and am met with three pairs of ruby red eyes staring back at me.

"Hey, you're alive!" Scar exclaims, appearing before me and inspecting me. I feel exposed under his gaze. "No injuries, nothing," he whispers. "I was right. You're not human, are you?"

"Really, Scar?" Hawke-eye chides. "You're making her uncomfortable. Give her some space." With a hunched back, Scar zips to the couch.

"Sorry." He sheepishly adds.

"I'm hungry."

"Okay, Syrus, do you have any blood in the fridge?" Hawke-eye asks, racing to the fridge.

"There should be, unless Rune ate all the packets again."

Hawke-eye shoves a cold packet into Zack's mouth. He grimaces at first before taking deep gulps. I relax and approach the other vampires in the lounge area.

I sit on the couch and wait for everyone to settle.

"Thanks for saving us. We couldn't do it on our own." I grimace, recalling all those guards dogpiling on us. Syrus waves his hand as he continues to read.

"It was no trouble! Killing a bunch of guards, stealing all their information and infecting their internal systems was a hella fun!" Scar gives a fanged grin.

"Why not burn the building down?" I snort.

"Way too much effort, and the cover up for a whole complex! Screw that."

"Besides, that would put more attention on us than needed," Hawk-eye shrugs.

"How did you rescue us?" Zack speaks with a mouth full of blood.

"Zack!" Scar scolds.

"I have my ways." Syrus shrugs his shoulders and a clawed hand emerges from the shadows, plopping a blood bag beside him. My mouth falls. Questioning if that was my tired brain, or a sudden fresh case of insanity.

An uncomfortable silence falls over us. Syrus' brothers stare at me, all looking like they are about to burst like an overfilled water balloon, their mouths contorted, eyes bulging with desperation. One Scar had already asked, but was desperate to know the answer to. Syrus, on the other hand, is unbothered, a book in his hand, eyes downcast, absorbing every word written on the page. Not caring if I have the answer or not.

"I'm half vampire." Silence. Everyone looks at Syrus and then back at me. He closes his book and places it down on the coffee table. He leaves the lounge, disappearing down the hall. We all look to each other in silence. The air becomes stifling as we wait.

Syrus returns with a laptop in hand and sits back in his original spot.

"Scar, found some files when we were busting you out," Syrus hands the machine to me. "So far I am the only to watch them, but it should give you some answers."

'*0402*' my blood runs cold as I recognise the numbers. My birthday. I open the file and unique documents and videos align by date. I click the very first video–'*interrogation.*'

The screen comes up black, but the date and time show on the bottom screen. Six months before the accident.

'*There's a child. One we've never seen before. An enigma.*'

'*What do you mean?*' Nic's voice rings in my ears.

'*This child could be our downfall or our saviour. She's a hybrid. Half Vampire, Half Human. One of a Kind.*'

'*That's impossible. Are the Parents?*'

'Human. Both of them are related to the child!'

'You better not be lying!'

I swallow down the lump forming in my throat and jump in my seat as I hear the gunshot ring out. Releasing a shaky breath, I close the laptop and place down on the coffee table.

"A hybrid, huh?" Hawke-eye clarifies, bewildered.

"At least we know what happened to the warlock that contacted us," Scar whispers.

I look at Syrus. The vampire watches me with an intense gaze.

"The only reason they wanted me in the first place." I clench my hands, gripping the fabric of my pants. "Killing my parents… ripping me away from my friends, my family… all because I'm some hybrid." my voice cracks, tears streaming down my face.

"Ceres," Zack whispers my name.

"We'll have to test this first. I don't trust their word just yet," Syrus deadpans. His eyes glow in the darkness. A power unfolds from the vampire, and the room grows eerily quiet.

Hawke-eye and Killer stiffen and watch their older brother closely. "But if he is speaking the truth. You would be one of a kind, an anomaly to the universe, and yet balance has not shifted." His words hang heavy in the air. I don't understand the implications, but now I know there is a balance, an order that must be maintained and I am an anomaly. If this balance hasn't shifted, what does my existence mean? Am I a sign of death? Will I cause destruction? Where will I find the answers? How can I? where do I start? "I wonder, are you here to maintain order or to be the downfall of our species? If it's the latter," shadowed creatures emerge from the floor beneath my feet and grab my ankles, another holds my arms behind my back, and another sharpens its claws around my neck. Syrus's fangs glint in the light, and an omnipresent aura emits from the vampire.

Zack trembles in fear, stuck in a lurch, wanting to jump in between Syrus and me but fearful of the vampire's repercussions and wanting to hide behind the older vampires beside him.

"You're not normal yourself," I shoot a glare at the older vampire, tears still falling down my face.

"Ridiculous as this sounds, but there is a monarchy in our society," Syrus makes clear.

"And you're the king," I finish for him. Syrus smiles and nods.

"As much as I hate my title, it is still my responsibility to ensure the survival of my species and the well-being of my family."

"Then go ahead."

"No! Syrus, please!" Zack shouts, shaking in his spot. The aura the king creates consumes the room. I can feel it seeping into my bones, but unaffected by its power. Zack shrinks back, hiding behind Scar, eyes wide with fear, his hands trembling as they grip on to Scar's shirt. The older vampires are still in their place, shifting uncomfortably as they look to their older brother. Their guarded pose speaks volumes. 'Don't mess with him.'

"You're not afraid to die?" I shake my head.

"What's the point now? Life was boring before all this happened, and now, figuring out Nic raised me to be some willing killing machine. It explains all the training, the arguments, the persistent push to go down a path I didn't want to go down in the first place, and I finally chose what I wanted to do, and I get punished." I grit. Taking a deep breath, I give the vampire a dark grin. "And besides, what are you going to do? A moral test, a personality questionnaire, tarot cards, palm readings? How are you going to decide I'm not dangerous?" I snarl feeling the beast claw its way through the desire to challenge. "Cause if there is some universal mumbo jumbo that's involved, and considering both my parents are human, you're right, it is impossible. Something would have taken me out as soon as I was born, but nothing happened. I'm still here." A small smile curls on Syrus's lips, a little laugh escapes from his nose.

"You've got guts," Syrus acknowledges. "I can see why he likes you." I finally break the staring contest to look at Zack. Hiding behind his hands. The shadows release me, pleased with the outcome. "Killer, take a sample and find out if they are telling the truth," Syrus orders, and his younger brother does so without question. He goes down the dark hallway and comes back with a kit. I question how long it has been there or whether this was planned from the start.

"Okay, just open your mouth," Killer instructs. I open my mouth, and he swabs the inside of my cheek. He then hands over a test tube with solvent inside. "Can you also spit into that for good measure?"

"At least it's not marrow," I spit into the tube. Killer frowns but remains silent.

"Tell me, Ceres, what do you want?" Syrus asks me.

I feel an out-of-body experience, as if a shock struck me in the chest and stopped my heart, throwing me off guard. So used to having a path laid out for me, I never considered having a choice. This is the first time someone has asked me what I wanted in life, what I want to do, and I know what I want, what I always wanted.

"I want to be free," I finish my thoughts out loud. Syrus smiles.

"Well, I have my proposition for you. You don't have to accept."

"I feel a 'but' coming on," I interject. Syrus snorts and shrugs.

"If you ever come after my family and the ones I hold dear, I will destroy you myself," he warns. I nod in agreement.

"Very well. What's the job?"

"The government hired Nic's company, and they will kill anything supernatural. Unlike us, we kill a particular type, known as ferals. These are humans who are not meant to be vampires, their souls devoid of a vampiric soul that marks one for our kind." Syrus looks to Zack and gives him a knowing smile. "Everyone has souls, and in this universe, our souls define what we are. A human possessing a vampire soul is called an Abeyant. Born human, waiting and seeking a vampire out to become whole, their true self. Your friend was one until we turned him." Zack looks away, struggling to maintain eye contact with me. "Humans who are mistakenly turned by our kin or by other ferals lose their soul and all there is left is the husk of a mindless beast. Unchecked, they create more and kill anything with a beating heart, a pest if you will. Certain covens hunt them to keep numbers down. I have a few members who do this, and I pay them for each head they bring. I will offer you the same."

"Why do you want to kill your own kind?" Syrus shakes his head.

"They're not," he bluntly states. "Everything has a balance. For example, made werewolves are mindless beasts. They transform under the full moon once a month unable to control themselves, unlike born werewolves who can control their shift at will. They have a lust for power, wanting to conquer and destroy other species." A growl rumbles to his throat. Before speaking once more, he takes a calming breath. "The magical community, humans born with magic, hide away, pretending the problems involving us don't involve them. Branding themselves as the pure species as they do not have defects–except the ones who turn to decay magic. This is all intertwined with the balance of the universe in our many worlds." My head starts to spin.

"Werewolves? Worlds? I heard that, right?"

"You heard correctly. Worlds, all unique in their own way, things you thought would never exist. Lands filled with magic, creatures of all kinds, eras remaining the same for centuries, different technologies, different walks of life. All are very different compared to this world, which is very dull, but it's nice apart from your government messing in our affairs," Syrus sighs. "It's a lot to take in, I understand." My head swims with the information dumped on me. Worlds, werewolves. A system, how many layers are there in the universe? There's so much I need to know.

"There is so much beneath the surface." Silence falls on us once more. How, how is any of this possible? What kind of magic mumbo jumbo am I hearing? Magic and supernatural forces can't be an explanation for everything, can it? If the universe is this deep, this big, then there might be a chance. "Then there's an answer to my existence." Syrus smiles. "What do I need to do?"

"You hunt down these ferals and kill them. It's as simple as that. You get to live a life you want and earn money for each feral you kill. Though you cannot kill vampires who aren't ferals, and don't worry, I'll teach you how to distinguish between the two."

"For someone who wanted to kill me, you are putting a lot of trust in me not to kill you." Syrus only snorts and shakes his head.

"Because I know you won't trust me unless I give you a reason to, and this offer is a build of that trust." I hate that he's right. I sigh, turning my gaze away from the vampire and staring at the view. Am I going into one cage to another?

"Do I have to give you an answer?"

"No." I snap my head back to the vampire. "You can take all the time you need. Even if you say no now, the offer will remain." I clench my fists. Uneasiness settles in my stomach. This has to be some kind of trap, a lie. No one is this lenient. "Come with me." He smiles.

Chapter 23

Syrus opens the door, revealing a spacious apartment overlooking the Brisbane River. Many would kill for this view. The price alone is enough to make any middle-income earner go broke. The condo itself has the bare essentials: a working fridge, oven, stove, furniture, and a TV. "While you're making your decision, you can stay here," Syrus states, opening the glass door to the balcony.

"People my age would give anything for a place like this," I remark, walking to the black granite counter. "Why are you offering this to me?"

"If you agree, you'll need to be close to the creatures you hunt. It would be tedious for you to travel back and forth."

"Shouldn't you be renting this out?"

"This place is for emergencies, till you find somewhere you desire. You can stay here for the time being and besides, dealing with tenants is a nuisance. I don't need another source of income."

"Considering you own the building, no surprise there," Zack blurts out, and Syrus can only stare at the young vampire with his icy gaze, telling him to be quiet. Zack ducks behind the counter. "Sorry."

"This is too much to take in." I feel my head thump between my skull.

"Don't pressure yourself too much; think about it first," Syrus assures. "I'll leave you two alone. I have other things to attend to." he leaves the apartment and closes the door behind him. My legs turn to jelly. Wanting to sit down, I head to the balcony, leaning against the glass panelling, breathing in the fresh air I so desperately need. Breathe in… Breathe out. Zack silently follows, sitting next to me, leaning against my shoulder. We sit in silence, letting the city's noise fill the void.

"So, what are you going to do?" Zack asks me. I remain silent and look up at the blue sky, watching the fluffy white clouds slowly drift by.

"Don't know…" I answer. "My original plan was surviving high school. Now I have all this to deal with." Zack stays quiet, his head resting on my shoulder. I look down and see his eyes slowly beginning to close. "I want to find my own way."

"Give it time," Zack yawns. "You don't have to make a decision now," he advises. I know, but gut tells me otherwise.

I reminisce over the last week. I had to fight for my life. Zack came to the rescue. The person who raised me betrayed me. All in the name of their cause.

"I can't believe it," I look back into the apartment. Zack turns his head to me, his eyes wide like saucers. "They cause all the chaos in my life, just so they can use me. All to make me a weapon and hunt down vampires."

"You don't have to. You're free," Zack assures me. I grimace and shake my head.

"Am I? I'm an anomaly in the universe. Will Syrus even let me go unchecked, or will I die by his hands?" Zack flashes his fangs in pure rage.

"He has to kill me first before he tries anything!" Zack shouts before he shamefully bows his head and takes an unneeded breath. "Sorry. No, he wouldn't... he knows how much you mean to me," Zack whispers, gently grasping my hand in his own. His hand isn't as cold to the touch as it used to be. It's warm, soft, comforting. "Do you have any plans after high school?" he pauses and then continues. "Except possibly accepting the offer."

"Nope. I have no plans, no path, just nothing." I shrug. This hollowed emptiness in my chest is filled with longing, loss, fear, and hopeless dreaming. I wish to embrace the parts of me, experience and feel. If only I could drop into the ocean and hope it would carry me away.

"I wanted to be free," I answer. "I want to go anywhere, be whoever I want to be, make my path and find a place to call my own. Working in a standard office building with regular working hours is not what I want. I don't want to bend over backward for someone's gain. I want to break my back for my benefit. My goal is to have the freedom to live my life without interference. Zack gives half a smile and gently pulls me into a hug from behind. His nose is in my hair, his powerful arms wrapped around me. "And now I have it, and I'm terrified."

"It's understandable. You've been through so much."

Chapter 24

"Congratulations on your graduation," Syrus smiles as I walk over the threshold. Before I can speak, Hawke-eye swiftly interrupts.

"Should have seen her, all blushing when I cheered for her. Took some really good photos too," he zips to Syrus' side to show him the photos. I cover my face and groan, feeling like I'm dying of embarrassment.

"Ooooo, let me see," Zack chimes in, racing to their side and gawking at the photos.

"Really?"

"What?" Hawke-eye responds innocently.

"It's just a graduation," I shrug. "It's no big deal."

"No big deal!" Zack gasps, his voice filled with disbelief. "It's a huge deal! You were ready to drop out so many times. I'm incredibly proud of you!" A blush creeps up my cheeks. I turn away from the vampires' intense gazes and look at the floor.

"Idiot."

"I take it all went smoothly then?" Syrus look to his brother.

"Yep, if Hidebound were to show, we were there waiting. Besides why would they make a scene?" Hawke-eye shrugs.

"Well then, this calls for a celebration," Syrus declares, rising from the couch. "Dinner, perhaps? I know the perfect place."

"It's fine, you don't have to-"

"Oh c'mon, let's celebrate!" Zack insists, pulling me into a hug.

"Ok, ok. Just a small one," I relent, giving in to their enthusiasm. Zack fist pumps the air and cheers around the apartment.

Zack and I sit on the balcony of my new place, overlooking the Brisbane River. We sit in peaceful silence, the city's chaotic noise below serving as our soundtrack.

"I'm not going to accept the offer," I announce suddenly. "I want to explore what other options are out there first."

"That's fair," he responds, his voice calm. "Do you have any plan in mind?" I shake my head.

"Find a job. Maybe travel."

"We could go to Europe together, and then maybe the States," Zack suggests excitedly. "Or maybe travel around the country first. I want to see the big banana," he adds, followed by laughter. His smile fades as he looks at my face. "What's wrong?"

Don't tie him down to your misery. Don't let him take responsibility for your happiness. Let him go, let him be happy.

"When, other than what happened in the last year, was the last time we were ever apart?" Zack pauses for a moment before responding.

"Primary school for the last few years before we went to the same high school," he answers. "But we tried to see each other nearly every weekend until Nic stepped in," Zack adds with a snarl.

"When other forces aren't stopping us, we are always together," I continue. "We lean on each other for support so much that when we are apart, we crumble." I swallow the lump forming in my throat.

"You're not making any sense," he shakes his head, confusion evident in his voice. "I thought… I thought we… you." His words become a jumbled mess. I gently place my hand on his, feeling him tremble under my touch.

"It's not that I don't care. I love you, I really do," I assure him, and Zack stops shaking. "But I feel like I would hurt you more if we got together, and I don't want that." I continue, rubbing his hand. "We need to stand on our own two feet. I want you to explore, take pictures of the world, and see it for what it is," I reason, and Zack shakes his head.

"We can explore the world together. Nic's not here to stop us anymore. We can be together!"

"Zack," I whisper, and the young vampire calms down, looking at me with puppy-dog eyes. "I want us to be two whole individuals, not two halves that make one. We need to stand strong and not crumble when apart."

"We can do that together, we can make that work!"

"Can we? Or will we fall into the same habits?" Zack remains silent, his grip tightening.

"Maybe," he croaks.

"Maybe," I echo. "But we need to do this. What we have isn't healthy." Zack's shoulders slump, and his intense gaze doesn't waver.

"Will we ever…" his voice falters.

"One day. But for now, I think it's best we go on our own paths. Discover ourselves, learn what we can, and come back stronger."

Zack leans his head on my shoulder, our hands still entwined, the wind gently blowing through his bangs, his eyes staring into the illuminated lights, lost in thought.

"I love you, Ceres," he murmurs, and a silent tear streaks down his cheek. I wrap my arms around him, holding my friend close, letting the numbing sensation take hold of my heart, easing the ache but unable to repair the cracks put in place. Burying my head in his shoulder, I let the silent tears leak down. "I love you too," I whisper into him.

Epilogue

"Everything packed?" I ask.

"Yep," Zack nods, adjusting his backpack. "I'm told I just need to bring my valuables. I can get clothes over there."

"I still don't understand why we're meeting in front of this old building," I grumble, gazing up at the brick structure in Fortitude Valley.

"Beats me. Scar said to meet him here, and he'll take me to Syrus' brothers in the UK," his gaze joining mine.

"Ready to head off!" Both of us jump as Scar approaches. I place my hand over my chest, trying to calm my racing heart.

A figure slowly emerges from the shadows cast by the building. I recognise the brown hair, the lifeless gaze, and the small, smug smile on his lips.

"How do you do that?" my mouth left agape.

"One of the many powers I possess," Syrus responds nonchalantly. "Give Lorens and the others my regards. It's been a while since I've spoken to them."

"Uh, yeah, I will," Zack replies, snapping out of his stupor and giving the vampire king an eager nod.

"Right!" Scar announces. "No time like the present!" He approaches the brick wall, glancing around his surroundings before opening his mouth. "London, UK, Aperio."

Magic sparks, and a door opens before us. It's like looking through a window, perfectly clear. On the other side is a dimly lit street, and I can feel the chill coming through.

"After you!" Scar announces.

Zack mirrors my surprise. He looks at me and then back at the door as if to say, 'You're seeing this too?' I nod. With a deep breath, he hugs me tight one last time.

"Have fun, learn lots of new things," I whisper. Zack holds me close one last time.

"I will. You too. I know we'll see each other again soon." Zack lets go and approaches the door. With careful steps, he crosses the threshold, relaxing once he's on the other side. Scar chuckles and follows. "See you later tonight, Syrus," he waves. "Claudre." The door closes.

"What the hell did I just see?"

"A door. You can't see the mark because you don't have the sight, but they're everywhere," Syrus answers.

"How do they work? Is it just to get to locations?" I touch the brickwork where the door once stood.

"Yes, and no," Syrus responds cryptically. "Best for you to know less. After all, you wanted a normal life, yes?" he smirks.

"Cheeky bastard," I mumble, but sigh afterward. "I'll find my own apartment once I have a job," I add.

"No need. You can stay as long as you want."

"What's the catch?"

"No catch. Consider it my way of keeping an eye on things. You may want a normal life, but I can't have a hybrid go unchecked," he glowers.

"Insurance policy, huh?" Syrus smiles. "Fine. Not like I was going to do anything drastic."

"True, but I'm not taking any chances," Syrus shrugs and disappears into the shadows once more, leaving me alone.

"Not that you're going to have any trouble," I mutter under my breath. "This is just the beginning, isn't it?" I ask the universe, a sense of anticipation mixed with trepidation settling in my chest.

The End?

About the Author

Belinda Topan is an author from QLD, Australia.

Belinda started writing when she was four years old. Her imagination has been a relentless source of inspiration, leading Belinda on thrilling journeys where she became the hero she always aspired to be.

She is passionate about all things vampire that are devoid of remorse, creatures unburdened by empathy for human life. The vampires Belinda has crafted possess a unique twist—they care to a certain extent, yet still embody the cruelty they are often depicted. Belinda chooses to base her stories here in Australia because she believes that her beloved home is always excluded in vampire stories or any supernatural narrative.

Belinda wants to express her heartfelt gratitude to all of you for your unwavering support along her creative journey.

Sunset

"What defines a monster? Is it their appearance – sharp teeth, eerie eyes, or rough skin? Or is it their actions, habits, and behaviour?"

These questions are explored as we journey to Ancient Rome where the head sorcerer makes a gruesome sacrifice in search of a particular soul. Syrus Valerius is the sole survivor, and he becomes the target of the people's ire.

Alexandros takes Syrus under his wing, and a young girl named Annabeth soon enters his life. Despite facing adversity and prejudice, Syrus grows into adulthood and continues to fight against the harsh words of the people. However, as his 21st birthday approaches, he fears that all his efforts may be in vain.

Sunrise

Rune has lost all hope and is ready to embrace death after living on the streets for years. But when he is approached by Syrus Valerius, a vampire who has wandered the earth for centuries, he is offered eternal life.

As a new vampire, Rune struggles to control his thirst for human blood and adapt to his new home. He must also navigate the complex dynamics of his relationship with Syrus.

However, Rune's troubled past resurfaces and threatens their newfound peace. In order to protect themselves, they must rely on the help of others and continue to learn and grow. Will they be able to overcome their past and secure their future together?

Living with Vampires

Three vampires. One human. A whole lot of chaos.

What could possibly go wrong?

Living with vampires is far from the glamorous fantasies we've been led to believe. Our heroine stumbles through the daily challenges of living with a trio of vampires who redefine the word dysfunctional. Endless bickering and clashes are just the tip of the iceberg. Not only does Valeria have to put up with their constant bickering and fighting, but also the never-ending stream of chaotic antics that ensue.

Our hero begins to document her experiences and her readers can't get enough of the crazy antics and bizarre encounters. Her audience becomes captivated, but as the blog gains popularity, it also attracts some dangerous attention.

Amidst the bedlam, a unique bond forms between our Valeria and her nocturnal roommates. Prepare to witness vampires in an entirely new light as their peculiar friendship unfolds before your eyes.

You'll laugh, you'll cry, you'll be on the edge of your seat waiting to see what happens next. Will our heroine survive? Will she be turned into a vampire herself?

www.ingramcontent.com/pod-product-compliance
Lightning Source LLC
Chambersburg PA
CBHW021013120726
47905CB00009B/2999